"Even if I do sleep with you, it doesn't mean I'm going to marry you."

"Before you start introducing conditions again," he suggested huskily, "you should consider that two can play at that game." Smiling fiercely down into her bewildered face, he elaborated. "I could, for instance, say if you won't marry me, I won't make love to you."

Every nerve in her body screamed out in protest at the suggestion.

"You're not serious!" She scanned his face for any sign that this was an empty threat, and found none. It was a very persuasive argument.

Though lacking much authentic Welsh blood, **KIM LAWRENCE**—from English/Irish stock—was born and brought up in north Wales. She returned there when she married, and her sons were both born on Anglesey, an island off the coast. Though not isolated, Anglesey is a little off the beaten track, but lively Dublin, which Kim loves, is only a short ferry ride away.

Today they live on the farm her husband was brought up on. Welsh is the first language of many people in this area, and Kim's husband and sons are all bilingual. She is having a lot of fun, not to mention a few headaches, trying to learn the language!

With small children, the unsocial hours of nursing weren't too attractive, so, encouraged by a husband who thinks she can do anything she sets her mind to, Kim tried her hand at writing. Always an avid Harlequin® reader, she felt it was natural for her to write a romance novel. Now she can't imagine doing anything else.

She is a keen gardener and cook, and enjoys running—often on the beach, because, since she lives on an island, the sea is never very far away. She is usually accompanied by her Jack Russell, Sprout—don't ask, it's a long story!

THE ITALIAN'S RUTHLESS MARRIAGE BARGAIN
KIM LAWRENCE

~ THE BILLIONAIRE'S CONVENIENT WIFE ~

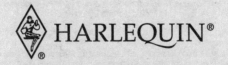

HARLEQUIN®

TORONTO • NEW YORK • LONDON
AMSTERDAM • PARIS • SYDNEY • HAMBURG
STOCKHOLM • ATHENS • TOKYO • MILAN • MADRID
PRAGUE • WARSAW • BUDAPEST • AUCKLAND

PLEASE RECYCLE · THIS PRODUCT IS RECYCLABLE

Recycling programs
for this product may
not exist in your area.

ISBN-13: 978-0-373-52709-0
ISBN-10:   0-373-52709-8

THE ITALIAN'S RUTHLESS MARRIAGE BARGAIN

First North American Publication 2009.

Previously published in the U.K. under the title
THE ITALIAN PLAYBOY'S PROPOSITION.

Copyright © 2003 by Kim Lawrence.

www.eHarlequin.com

Printed in U.S.A.

THE ITALIAN'S RUTHLESS
MARRIAGE BARGAIN

CHAPTER ONE

REFERRING to his notes occasionally, Tom Trent spoke at length. He knew the man who had had him flown back from his Stateside holiday on Concorde for this meeting well enough to know he wouldn't want him to pull his punches, and he didn't.

Elbows set on the mahogany desktop, long brown fingers steepled, the figure behind the desk listened Tom out in silence. Tom could only imagine how he was feeling, for his dark patrician features gave no clue whatsoever of what was going on in his mind—a mind that was the sharpest that Tom, who was no intellectual slouch himself, had ever encountered.

'So that's about it, then,' Tom concluded leaning back in his seat.

Luca didn't respond immediately; instead he rose to his feet in one fluid motion. At six feet five fit inches of solid bone and muscle he made an imposing figure. His dark, contemplative gaze rested on his friend for several moments before he sighed and began to pace the room.

As he watched the languid, loose-limbed tread of the tall man Tom, not a person renown for his imaginative flights, found the image of a sleek panther, its natural instincts confined within cage bars, appear in his head.

After a second circuit of the room Luca came to halt by the big desk and, placing his hands palm down on the gleaming surface, he leant towards the other man. The thick curling eyelashes, which Tom's own wife had declared to be sinfully sexy, lifted from sharp, jutting cheekbones and Tom found himself on the receiving end of the famous Di Rossi stare. It wasn't a comfortable place to be.

'So what you're saying is the only foolproof way to avoid a custody battle would be for me to find a wife, preferably one who has a child of her own?'

Tom shook his head. It was typical of Luca to condense thirty minutes' worth of complicated legal explanation in one sentence, but then Gianluca Di Rossi was not a man who used two words when one would do. Like his words, his actions too were always focused and to the point.

Small talk was not Luca's thing!

The flip side of this was that when other people wrote memos and had endless meetings Luca acted. Making decisions was not something that Luca agonised about; he didn't feel the need for other people to validate his actions or anyone else to blame when those actions had consequences. So the fact that some people called him reckless and others called him inspired did not matter to him.

So far his supreme self-belief had been more than justified by the spectacular success of the empire he had carved out of nothing.

'Well, I hadn't thought of it that way, but a ready-made family would really damage their case, if not kill it stone-dead. If you're going to interview for the job, a couple of kids, one of each would be good.'

His humour produced no lightening of the sombre, brooding expression in the dark penetrating eyes fixed unblinking on his face, nor any relaxation of the taut lines in Luca's lean, hard face. But then, Tom conceded, feeling inexcusably in-sensitive, I wouldn't feel inclined to laugh at my pathetic wit-ticisms if someone were trying to take my kid off me.

'A ready-made family…' Luca repeated slowly.

'Bad joke, but it's not like I'm telling you anything you didn't already know.'

'Sometimes it takes someone else to point out the obvious before you see what's staring you straight in the face,' Luca observed somewhat enigmatically before folding his long, lean length into his chair once more.

Hands rested lightly on the leather arm-rests, he tilted the head-rest back and stared up at the high ceiling. The London office of Di Rossi International having recently moved from its cramped modern offices to this Georgian terrace, which had been restored with meticulous attention being paid to pe-riod detail and very little to cost, he found himself looking at some pretty fine plaster mouldings.

The shadow cast by the downward sweep of Luca's lashes effectively concealed his deep-set eyes and expression from the other man. To all intents and purposes he appeared re-laxed, but as people over the years had learnt, frequently to their cost, with Luca appearances could be deceptive.

'Di Rossi is at his most dangerous when cornered!' a shrewd economic analyst had once written. This went tenfold for his personal life, which he guarded jealously. And at that moment his personal life was under attack.

'You could always put an advert in the personal column. All right,' Tom conceded quickly with a grimace, 'that wasn't funny either. 'But lighten up, it's not like I'm actually sug-gesting you go out and get married! For one thing they don't stand a chance in hell of winning the case.'

'But they will make sure my name is dragged through the mud.'

'The negative effect on the company will only be temporary Luca,' Tom was quick to point out soothingly. 'And that's not just spin, I promise you. Di Rossi is far too solid in the market-place to suffer any long-term damage from a court case.'

One sardonic brow arched. 'Your concern for my financial interests is laudable.' The accented drawl became diamond-hard as he added, 'However, the damage on Valentina might not be so temporary.'

Tom winced. 'Ah, God, yes, what was I thinking about? Sorry, Luca.'

Luca lifted his head. 'Why?'

Tom blinked and looked nonplussed by this abrupt question. 'Why what?' he queried, his manner guarded.

'Why should I not get married?'

'You're not serious!' Again he received the look. 'Well, other than the odd hundred or so reasons that spring to mind, it would be totally—'

'Necessary, according to you,' Luca interjected seamlessly. 'If I want to kill off the case before it gets to court. And I'd do anything it takes to protect Valentina from being dragged through that. Being exposed to those vultures.'

Looking into those implacable eyes, Tom realised this was no figure of speech. In a world where people frequently said things they didn't mean for effect, it had taken him some time to catch onto the fact that when Luca said something that was exactly what he meant!

It was the lawyer who felt the need to break the ensuing heavy silence.

'To them it must seem you moved her to England to deliberately make it harder for them to have access…' he suggested tentatively.

Luca ran a hand over his smooth shaven chiselled jaw and gave a wolfish smile. 'I did.'

'Then when you refused to give them unaccompanied access—' Tom shrugged '—you *must* have known how they'd react. Natalia Corradi hates you, Luca, and Valentina is her granddaughter.'

'And *my* daughter,' Luca flashed back, a lick of flame in his glittering eyes that made his friend draw back in his seat.

'Don't kill the messenger, mate,' he pleaded, holding out his hands palm upwards in pacific gesture.

The muscles in Luca's brown throat worked as he swallowed. The strong lines of his face were set in stone by the time he had regained his composure.

'Did I tell you what I heard her saying to Valentina?' he asked in a soft voice.

'No, Luca.'

'Her *loving* grandmother was telling her what a shame it was she is not as beautiful and talented as her mother was. Telling her that if she had never been born her mother would not be dead.' He drew a deep breath that expanded his powerful chest. '*Dio*…Tom, what was I to do?'

Tom, who was deeply shocked by these revelations, shrugged weakly.

'Who knows how long she has been dropping this poison in Valentina's ears? I will not let it happen to my daughter. I will not permit history to repeat itself,' he added half to himself. 'The woman, she has no feelings for the child,' he stated emphatically, adding the wry rider, 'at least not as you or I understand it. For her Valentina is a weapon to punish me.'

Once more he rose to his feet, grim determination in every line of his tall and vital figure. 'I have taken her contempt and vitriol over the years—it is of no matter to me.' He shrugged. 'But she has overstepped the mark this time. Valentina's needs must be considered above all else.'

'They'll say it is in Valentina's interests to be brought up within a loving family,' his friend pointed out gently. 'They will try and paint you as a…'

'Work-obsessed womaniser, I know.' His tight smile held self-mockery. 'I suppose the Erica factor is going to come into it?'

Tom nodded unhappily.

'And if I had sued the newspaper for libel as you, my friend, suggested at the time…?'

'Considering you had Erica admitting on tape that the bruise was nothing but clever make-up I still think you should have exposed her publicly at the very least, but then I don't have your gentlemanly code,' he admitted drily. 'Don't beat yourself up over that, Luca, it's easy to be wise in hindsight, but, yes, your refusal to defend yourself against those ludicrous accusations is going to look bad.'

'Oh, but you forget there were no accusations—in fact the beautiful victim bravely denied I had laid a finger on her, if you recall—'

Tom looked uncomfortable. 'Let's concentrate on things we *can* do something about,' he suggested. 'It's the male household factor that is a major stumbling block. The fact there is no female role model except for your…' He paused, looking awkward.

'My *women*?' Luca bit back with a hard, satirical smile.

The other man sighed. 'You can forget about your personal life being sacrosanct if this thing comes to court, Luca. You'll have to be prepared to have your love life dissected.'

'I am not a monk,' he admitted calmly. 'However, my love life is not nearly as interesting as the press would have you believe.'

A laugh was wrenched from the lawyer. 'If I don't believe you, Luca, how do you expect to convince a court? And have you thought how Carlo is going to look to a judge? I mean, *I* know he's a great chap but, let's face it, he's not most people's idea of a nanny. And then there's the matter of his record.'

'Carlo stays.' There was no room for negotiation in Luca's flat response and Tom, who knew personally of Luca's unswerving loyalty to his friends, did not argue the point. 'But I can—' The intercom on his desk buzzed and Luca's dark brows drew together in a frown. When he spoke into the offending machine his tone was terse and impatient.

'I thought,' he intoned coldly, 'that I said I didn't want—' He stopped and listened to whatever was being said and sighed. 'All right, tell him I'll ring back in five minutes.' He turned to the lawyer. 'Sorry about this, Tom, but it's Marco. He's got a problem.'

And when Marco had a problem he always turned to his half-brother. Tom couldn't prevent the look of disapproval that spread across his face. It was inexplicable to him that Luca, who did not tolerate fools gladly, should have such a fondness for his charming but feckless half-brother.

Luca saw the play of expression on his friend's face. 'You don't like Marco do you?'

'Anyone *normal* would resent a half-brother who is favoured so unfairly, Luca.'

Luca's severe features relaxed slightly as a thoughtful expression slid into his silver-shot dark eyes. 'Has it ever occurred to you that being considered incapable of doing anything wrong and supremely talented in all things by one's parents is not an easy role to fill for anyone with the normal degree of human weaknesses?'

'Well, Marco's got his fair share of those,' Tom conceded with a dry laugh. 'But to be honest, Luca, I think it's more of a *burden* to have your achievements, not only go totally unrecognised by your family, but resented,' he added, unable to repress his indignation on his friend's behalf.

'I do not seek anyone's approval,' Luca declared with chilling hauteur, which would have repressed nine men out of ten.

Tom, the tenth, shook his head. 'God, but you're an arrogant beggar!'

An unexpected grin of immense charm totally transformed the billionaire's dark features. 'That's seemed to be the general consensus,' Luca agreed drily. 'I'll ring you later,' he added as the other man moved towards the door.

'Are you going back to the house tonight? The renovations are completed?'

'They are, but we're staying in Marco's apartment for a few nights. I didn't say, Tom, but I am sorry to drag you away from Cape Cod.'

'I forgive you, but Alice might not.' Tom smiled. 'Luca, is there anything you want me to do in the meantime?'

'You could make up a list of possible brides.'

This comment made the other man pause as he reached for the door handle. 'I've known you ten years, Luca, and I still can't tell when you're joking.'

'I've never been more serious in my life, Thomas.'

'Mum, you've *got* to help me!'

'You expect me to drop everything, Jude?' There was a note of laboured incredulity in Lyn Lucas's husky voice that didn't quite ring true. 'Just like that!'

Appealing to her mother's maternal instincts always had been a long shot. 'There's a first time for everything,' Jude muttered, rueful affection in her stressed voice.

'What was that, Jude?'

'Nothing.' She took a deep breath and swallowed her pride. If begging was what it took she was prepared to beg; things were really that desperate. 'Listen, Mum, I wouldn't ask unless this was an emergency.'

'And if it were an emergency I would quite naturally be there for you,' Lyn returned serenely. 'But really, Jude, don't you think you're just a tad over the top with the drama, darling? They're only three little children…just how much trouble can they be?'

'How much? How *much*?' Jude standing in the middle of her open-plan living room, *once* a tribute to tasteful minimalism, took a deep steadying breath. 'Where,' she asked as the weight of her failure oppressed her, 'shall I start? Oh, God, Mum, it's not *them*, it's *me*!'

The logical part of her knew she was wasting her breath. How could you explain to someone whose idea of hands-on parenting was giving her teenage daughter charge accounts and a car?

When they'd been younger a long series of nannies had made sure she and David had only ever been produced for parental inspection when they'd been freshly scrubbed and on their best behaviour. As soon as it had been possible they had been shipped off to boarding-school. That, she mused, was probably why they'd ended up being so close.

'The children need someone who knows what they're doing,' she began in a frustrated tone when from the corner of her eye she caught movement. 'Hold on a minute, Mum,' she grunted, diving to retrieve a bottle of hair conditioner before the five-year-old could apply it to the blond curls of her sleeping baby sister.

'No, Sophia, that's Aunty Jude's.' Jude was frustrated to see her firm but reasonable remonstration had no visible effect on the five-year-old. Maybe it's not what I say but the way I say it.

'No!'

'Don't shout, Sophia, you'll wake Amy,' Jude pleaded, giving an anguished glance at the baby who stirred sleepily.

The little girl finally relinquished the bottle upon being offered a chocolate biscuit in exchange. You didn't have to be a trained clinical psychologist like herself to know bribery wasn't generally recommended as a method of child discipline, but Jude was frankly past caring about such niceties.

David, a dentist, would have been horrified by her breaking his draconian 'no sweeties or chocolate' edict; a great tide of sadness that had physical heaviness washed over her as she thought of her brother. David wasn't here to protect his children's teeth and neither was his wife, Sam. They had been killed the previous month when their car had gone through the central reservation on the motorway and collided head-on with a lorry.

When no other explanation for the accident had been forthcoming the inquest into the tragic deaths had concluded it was most likely the driver had fallen asleep at the wheel. The driver—*David*, her brother.

She knew all about the stages of the grieving process. Should that be helping? Jude didn't know. She just knew that she didn't have time to grieve, not yet. Right now her priority had to be three little children who needed a lot of love and understanding and the best way to do that seemed to be not trying to look more than a day ahead. If she did, the sense of her total inadequacy for the task that had been thrust upon her paralysed her.

She had loved being *Aunty* Jude, who could spoil and indulge them before handing them back at the end of the day. Having total responsibility was quite another matter, as she was learning!

She wanted to make the children feel safe and secure after their little world had been blown apart, but it was hard when she was scared herself. Scared because for the first time in her life something wasn't coming easy. She was failing at something, and this *something* wasn't an exam or a job. You could resit an exam or change a job, but where children's lives were concerned you didn't get to go back and try again.

Lately she'd begun to wonder if children, like animals, could smell fear. Well, whatever the reason, this brood had decided about ten seconds after they'd arrived that they didn't have to do as she asked.

I have to face it my mothering instincts are dreadful, she decided dully. Somewhat ironic, not to mention embarrassing, for the author of the catchily entitled *Parenting Skills for Beginners*.

With a token, 'Don't do that, sweetheart,' to Sophia, who was smearing chocolatey fingerprints all over her new cream sofa, she wearily raised the receiver to her ear in time to hear her mother say—

'What can they have done that is so bad? The twins are only three—'

'Five, Mum. The twins are five and Amy is eighteen months,' Jude reminded her mother wearily. 'And *they've* not done anything.' How could she explain to her literally minded mother that it wasn't the paintwork or the broken items she was worried about? That she hardly ever thought about the time when she had enjoyed coming back to her flat, kicking off her shoes and shutting the rest of the world out. 'Amy cries for her mum, and Sophia has nightmares, and Joseph—he *doesn't* cry.'

'Well, they've just lost their parents, Jude, what do you expect?'

'I know…I know, but it's not just that. It's this place, it's really hard to contain and amuse three children under six in a one-bedroomed apartment, Mum. I need somewhere with a garden?' she ended on a hopeful note.

Her mother had stayed in the family home after the divorce, a rambling Edwardian house on the edge of a picture-postcard village set in two acres of child-friendly gardens.

'Five is a delightful age, Jude,' replied the children's doting but absent grandmother with a catch in her voice. 'And I'd *love* for you all to come and stay here—'

'You don't know how glad I—'

'But unfortunately I have a meeting in New York this Friday and then guests next week. David,' she recalled huskily, 'was so sweet when he was five, so bright, so enquiring and so innocent…' Her voice dissolved into tears. 'I don't know how you can ask me to help when I'm suffering so much,' she reproached. 'And work is my only solace, you know that, Jude.

'They were such a lovely couple,' Lyn Lucas continued with a sigh. 'With everything to look forward to. 'Why them?'

Jude could only shake her head; her throat ached with unshed tears as she thought of her brother and his wife.

'I can't do this, Mum,' she whispered miserably down the phone. 'I'm messing up big time.'

'Well, David must have thought you could or he wouldn't have named you as the children's guardian,' came the bracing response.

'I doubt he expected I'd ever be put to the test,' Jude retorted sadly.

'Well, you have, and you'll just have to get on with it. It'll be a lot easier when you've sold the flat and bought something more sensible,' her mother continued. 'A nice little place in the country somewhere,' she mused as she conjured a picture of domestic bliss.

'I hate to ruin the roses-around-the-door scenario, but I have to live where the work is, Mum.' Thankfully they were being really good about giving her time off at the university where she lectured, so that was one less thing for her to worry about right now.

'Is all this about your job, Jude? I must say I'm disappointed in you, but not surprised.' Lyn sighed. 'You always have had a selfish streak. I mean, there's nothing *wrong* with a women having a career, but I would have thought under the circumstances that you would have been prepared to make a little sacrifice.'

This breathtaking piece of hypocrisy coming from a mother who had never made a parents' evening or sports day in her life left Jude momentarily speechless.

'This isn't about my job, Mum,' she managed finally. 'Though financially I do have to work,' she added drily. 'I'm good at my job. I'm not good at—'

'There's no such thing as the perfect parent, Jude,' her mother interrupted. 'Your problem is you're a perfectionist; you always have been. You don't like situations you can't control, or people. Just look at your boyfriends.'

'Must we?'

'Not a single one of them had an opinion of his own.'

'That's a gross exaggeration, Mother,' Jude retorted indignantly. 'I'm just not attracted to men who order dinner for me.'

For a liberated woman her mother had some very old-fashioned views of men. After her father had gone to live abroad she and David had found a new 'uncle' in residence every holiday they'd come home. The only thing they'd had in common beside their short shelf-lives had been their overbearing personalities.

'I've lost track,' she said, pressing her fingers to the pulse spots on her temple where the throbbing headache was building. 'Why exactly is my taste in men relevant to you refusing to help me?'

'Children are not predictable, Jude.'

'I'd noticed.'

'You have to be flexible and compromise.'

Jude was just too tired to fight. 'I'll try,' she promised.

'Good girl. It's just a pity that you haven't got a husband yet, because, let's face it, no man's going to look twice at a girl who comes with a ready-made family of three.' And on that cheery note, Jude thought, shaking her head slowly from side to side. My mum really is a one-off, which is probably just as well!

'Now, if there's anything you need just ask.'

And you'll be there for me so long as it doesn't interfere with a bridge game. 'Thanks, Mum.'

CHAPTER TWO

JUDE put down the phone and slumped down on the sofa amongst the biscuit crumbs and building blocks. The appeal to her mother had not had the outcome she had hoped for but Lyn's rather abrasive style had helped her get things back in perspective.

If I could have the last five minutes back, she reflected, I wouldn't have made that phone call. She gave a philosophical shrug. So I wimped out! This is not really that surprising, all things considered. I'm exhausted, I've lost my brother and I've become a mother of three almost overnight. Maybe I shouldn't be so tough on me?

Mum's right, she thought, squaring her shoulders, I need to stop bleating and get on with it. After all, there are plenty of single mothers out there who have it a lot worse than me and actually, Jude, girl, you're not doing so bad.

Her natural optimism and strength of character began to reassert itself as she sat there making the most of the moment of peace. Soon enough bedlam would break out once more; best to enjoy the moment whilst it lasted. Her affectionate glance slid to where Amy was sleeping—they really were delicious when then were asleep—and Sophia was sitting cross-legged on the rug crayoning and Joseph was…?

Where was Joseph?

When had she last seen Joseph, or heard his voice…?

Suddenly the silence seemed ominous. The mega dose of adrenaline suddenly introduced into her bloodstream wiped away the last dregs of tiredness. Revitalised and terrified, she levered herself up and ran into her bedroom, which had been transformed for the duration into a nursery. It was empty. The bathroom produced similar results. There weren't many places in the bijou flat that would conceal even a small child.

Heart racing, a sick feeling of dread curdling in the pit of her churning stomach, Jude raced back into the living room.

'Do you know where Joseph is, Sophia?' Don't scare her, don't scare her, Jude, she told herself, trying hard to keep the panicky tremor from her voice as she appealed to his twin.

'Yes,' the little girl replied without looking up.

Jude fought hard not to scream with frustration. She was about one heartbeat away from total panic. 'Where is he, Sophia? Where is Joseph?'

The little girl lifted her head and brushed a soft curl from her grubby forehead with her equally chubby forearm. 'He's gone to see the nice man with the computer game.'

Jude dropped to her knees beside the child. 'He's gone to see Marco?' she repeated with a note of hope in her voice.

Sophia nodded, her attention on the picture she was drawing. 'We like Marco, he's nice.'

Jude nodded, her thoughts racing. Illogically she was sure her nephew would be safe with Marco, even if the handsome occupant of the impossibly plush penthouse apartment upstairs did seem a little feckless at times.

Actually most of the apartments were plush to a greater or lesser extent—she occupied one of the token modestly priced apartments the builders had been forced to include in their project to satisfy local planning restrictions.

If only Joseph had got to Marco's apartment safely.

She couldn't let herself think about him not doing so. She couldn't bear to think about the little boy lost and alone. You heard such terrible stories…no, don't go there, Jude…focus, girl!

God! When she found that boy she was never going to let him out of her sight for a single second! If necessary she was going to superglue him to her side. Silently praying it actually would be that simple, she began to unstrap the sleeping baby from her reclining rocker seat.

'Come on, Sophia,' she said, turning to the little girl. 'We'll go and get Joseph for his lunch,' she added brightly. Her mental barriers were keeping the nightmare 'what ifs' at bay…just!

'That's it, Amy, we're going to take a little walk,' she told the drowsy baby as she lifted her into her arms.

'I don't want to go…' The little girl's mutinous response was almost drowned out by Amy, who had begun to loudly protest at being so rudely woken from her nap.

'Now!' Jude was as much surprised as relieved when the little girl responded without any further argument to her forceful command.

She was halfway to the door, her free hand tightly wrapped about the child's, when there was a loud, imperative knock on the door.

Jude ran across the room and flung the door wide.

'Aunty Jude!'

'Joseph!' To her relief her nephew looked none the worse for his experience, in fact he looked pretty pleased with himself.

Thank you, God and thank you, Marco! The closer her gaze got to the face of the man upon whose strong shoulders her nephew was perched, the more strained her beaming smile of gratitude became.

They had to travel a long way to get there, which may have accounted for the falling-off-a-tall-building suicide dive her stomach went into. At a conservative estimate he was six four, with a hard, athletically lean body under the superbly cut suit he wore. The jacket hung open to reveal a washboard-flat belly and lean, snaky hips. He had legs that went on forever to perfectly balance the magnificent shoulders.

When she had finally worked her way up to his face her exploration stalled and her smile vanished as her gaze locked onto a pair of spectacular midnight eyes.

This is more than surreal!

Of course she knew who he was—only someone who had spent the last few years in a coma or a convent would not have instantly recognised those dark, classically proportioned features.

It was easy to see why the camera loved the enigmatic, impenetrable deep-set eyes, sculpted, razor-sharp cheekbones, strong, mobile mouth and that glorious golden Mediterranean colouring. Unlike normal mortals, the closer you got, the better he looked. This guy didn't have a bad angle or need special lighting, he was about as close to flawless as you got.

Strangely, faced with this flesh and blood Adonis what hit Jude most forcibly was not his incredible face or scrumptious body, but what the lens had not been able to capture—the man exuded his own personal force field of raw, undiluted sexuality!

Jude, standing up close and personal, not *literally* obviously—now there was a thought—felt her stomach muscles quiver as she got a full dose of what he had in abundance. The impact was like walking into a solid wall. Staring up at him too dazed to hide her shock, Jude realised that what he exuded actually had little to do with his perfect bone structure, eyelashes long enough to make a girl weep or his wide, sensual mouth—though they naturally didn't do any harm!—but the innate sexuality of a virile male animal at the peak of his powers.

And, my God, doesn't he know it? she thought, her nose

wrinkled slightly with distaste. She found this brand of self-assurance not only disconcerting, but unattractive. He was the visual equivalent for her of someone scraping a nail down a blackboard.

She couldn't think of one reason, but there was probably a perfectly simple one, to explain why her nephew was sitting on the shoulders of The World's Most Notorious Playboy. One tabloid had stuck him with the title a couple of years back when it had run the personal story, complete with the obligatory salacious details, of a supermodel girlfriend he had ignominiously dumped.

The nickname had stuck and if half the things the girl had claimed were true it was well deserved she thought disapprovingly. She was no prude but *really*…! Jude felt heat travel over her skin as she recalled claims of his insatiable nature…did people really do things like that?

The stories of his sordid sexual exploits had actually done him no real harm—when had it done a man harm to be labelled a superstud? she thought cynically. What had actually done the damage to his reputation had been the dramatic black eye the model had been sporting in front of the cameras when interviewed. When asked she had instantly disclaimed that darling Luca had done it, but very few had believed her and suddenly people had been popping out of the woodwork with stories that seemed to give credence to his allegedly violent nature. Though significantly none of those stories had originated from previous lovers, who rubbished the reports.

Her protective instincts came on full alert.

'You're not Marco!' she heard herself exclaim accusingly.

Marco, with his bold eyes and warm smile, was handsome, and until she'd met this man she'd had him in her mental file marked 'attractive, predatory and dangerous.' Meeting this man had Jude rapidly redefining her definitions of predatory and dangerous!

'He's Luca!' Joseph announced importantly.

He's devastating! *Please let me not have said that out loud.*

'Are you all right, Joseph? You're not hurt or anything?' If she could have reached she would have yanked him down from those broad shoulders, but Amy was still nestled in her arms.

The man turned his head slightly, giving Jude a view of his perfect profile, and said something to the child that made the little boy laugh and ruffle the man's sleek hair with chubby fingers.

Jude, who was trying so hard to act as if she were totally cool about discovering a billionaire playboy on her doorstep that she was basically dumb, envied the child his naturalness.

A dreamy, unfocused expression slid into her wide-spaced eyes as she found herself speculating about what it might feel like to slide her own fingers into that thick, glossy… Without warning the muscles of her stomach tightened, making her gasp.

This was not a man a girl could let her imagination run wild around; fortunately she was not a girl who had any trouble keeping her imagination under control. And I thought I was too tired ever to even think of sex again. I guess we all have our breaking-point.

He turned his head suddenly and Jude froze.

'The child is, as you can see, unharmed.'

There was no evidence of the warmth she thought she had seen in his face as he'd spoken to Joseph; his eyes were drilled into her like knives.

'Thank you for returning him safely.'

Luca slipped Joseph off his shoulders in one smooth motion. She noticed that the expensive fabric of his perfectly cut dark grey suit fell back into place without a crease across his back as he straightened up.

She dropped on her knees beside the boy and hugged him with her one free arm, juggling Amy in the other. Blinking away the tears that filled her eyes, she rose to her feet. 'Go along inside, Joseph,' she bade huskily, all thoughts of remonstrance washed away by relief.

'Right then, thanks again,' Jude mumbled, guiltily avoiding contact with those unnerving dark eyes. He probably took being lusted after as no more than his due, but she was deeply embarrassed by her wayward imagination.

The awkward silence stretched, at least awkward on her part—she doubted this man had ever felt awkward in his life. He was assured down to his fingertips, one set of which was at that moment impatiently brushing a strand of dark hair from his broad, intelligent brow. As she followed the gesture with her eyes Jude discovered that his elegant, shapely hands with their long, tapering fingers exerted a strange fascination that made it difficult for her to drag her gaze away.

When she finally did so she could feel the dampness of nervous perspiration sticking her tee shirt to her back.

'I'd ask you to come in but—'

'You are a—*friend* of my brother's?' Mingled with the suspicion there was a note of cynical resignation in his voice, which passed Jude, who couldn't think about much beyond her overriding desire to get rid of this disturbing man, clear by.

He clearly expected her to say something; she wanted to say something, something that would draw a firm line under this incident. Unfortunately her brain chose that moment to disconnect with her vocal cords.

One strongly defined ebony brow arched when she remained dumb. The longer the silence stretched, the harder it was to fill. Frustration welled inside her as she stood there as if she were some tongue-tied, awestruck teenager rather than a responsible, mature career woman.

His deep, sexily accented voice was part of the problem. Even after he'd stopped speaking it continued to vibrate in a strange way through her body. Despising her susceptibility to his sexy vibes, she forced herself to concentrate.

'Marco?' she finally managed.

Marco was a Di Rossi? Well, of course she knew he was, but she hadn't previously made the connection with the incredibly wealthy Gianluca Di Rossi. For starters Marco, like many Italians of Northern extract was blond and secondly he didn't go around acting as if he had been born into one of the oldest Italian families, unlike his brother, who seemed very conscious of his blue blood not to mention his own importance.

The Di Rossis had been born with everything except money: impeccable lineage, enviable connections, a crumbling historic *palazzo* in Venice and a second home in Umbria surrounded by a neglected estate. Now thanks to Luca they had the money too—pots of the stuff. Or at least Luca did, but if the sort of clothes Marco wore and car he drove were anything to go by the elder brother's wealth was enjoyed by the entire family.

There were numerous theories, the darker even hinting at underworld connections, about how he'd made his first million before he was twenty-two, but nobody seemed to know for sure. There was no mystery about the source of his wealth these days—his international interests were diverse, ranging from a string of hotels to his own airline. Luca had an ability to read the market that some financial observers considered to border on the supernatural.

Being left standing on a doorstep was a first for Luca, who had decided it was concern for the child that stopped him from turning around. He was beginning to think the brunette was not only the owner of the most sultry mouth he had ever seen, but stupid.

With a less vacant expression on her face she would probably be quite attractive. Actually almost beautiful, he mentally corrected, re-evaluating the small, appealing face with its tip-tilted nose, luminous eyes and wilful mouth upturned to him—if, that was, you were prepared to overlook the slight irregularity of the features and the angularity of her small, determined chin.

The evidence that she had recently shed tears—she had the sort of pale, almost translucent complexion that showed such things—did not stir his pity. In Luca's considered opinion it was the children some parent had unwisely committed to her care that deserved his sympathy.

Doubtless her attention had been divided between her charges, watching daytime television and talking to her boyfriend on the phone—the children coming a poor second, he thought scornfully.

As he visualised the likely scenario that had led to a small, defenceless child wandering alone in the building his contempt for the girl and the persons who had left their children in the charge of the youthful incompetent escalated.

'You are a *friend* of my brother?' Luca disliked repeating himself almost as much as he disliked the idea of this girl knowing his brother, who was renown for his inability to see beyond a pretty face and was, despite some very severe lessons on what *not* considering the consequences of his actions resulted in, painfully impulsive.

'*Friend…?*' Even as she echoed the word the not-so-subtle emphasis he placed on the word and the contemptuous curl of his lip belatedly hit her. *Friend* in this instance was clearly a euphemism for lover and from his expression it was equally clear that Luca Di Rossi didn't much like the idea of his brother slumming it.

Angry spots of colour appeared on her cheeks as Jude felt

a surge of anger. She lifted her chin. Marco, with his easy charm and pleasing manner, had made it plain that he was interested, but she wasn't, and now it was academic—as her mum had said, no man wanted a woman who came with three small children.

Actually, now she came to think of it the one time she had seen Marco since the children had arrived he hadn't asked her out, whereas previously he had never let an opportunity pass. Clearly his alleged devotion had limits, Jude thought in amusement, but she was prepared to forgive him this lack of staying power because he had been so nice to the kids, but then Italians were reputed to be dotty about children. Though, she thought, angling a glance up at the dark, arrogant features of the man looking down his nose at her, there had to be exceptions.

So no need whatever for Marco's autocratic, stuck-up brother to know that the chances of her developing the sort of *friendship* he was talking about with the younger Di Rossi was nil—let him worry a little.

She pretended to consider the matter. 'I think that would be overstating it…' she lowered her eyes and looked up at him through her lashes with a coy smile '…for the moment…'

Luca watched with narrowed eyes as she gave a complacent toss of her head that sent the glossy curls dancing. The action completed the message in her words, namely that it would only take a click of her fingers to change that situation.

Not stupid after all, or beautiful, but she had something more dangerous than beauty—she oozed sex appeal. A man looked at her mouth and wanted to kiss it, at her body and imagined it minus clothes. Maybe there was not a world-class intellect lurking behind those gold-shot eyes, but, he thought cynically, when you combined a face and body like hers with a degree of animal cunning you didn't need to be a genius to get what you wanted.

The question was did she want Marco? Not that this was a scenario he would countenance.

Her confidence was, he conceded as his eyes slid slowly over the firm curves of her taut, youthful body, most probably justified. Her body might not be lush enough for some men's taste, but they would be in the minority. Luca had come across this sort of female before, the sort that possessed a sensuality that drew men like the proverbial moths to the flame, the sort that liked to control a man with sex.

During the few moments it took him to draw these conclusions the subject of his conjecture, oblivious to the opinion he had formed of her, was occupied with trying to soothe Amy who, having apparently been almost as gobsmacked by the sight of Luca Di Rossi on the doorstep as her aunt, had recovered her voice.

Amy, who was clearly destined to be a future diva, had a staggering vocal range.

When Jude looked up she found the not-so-friendly neighbourhood billionaire playboy was watching her with a peculiar intensity. There was absolutely no discernible expression in those heavy-lidded midnight eyes, but Jude was suddenly painfully conscious of her dishevelled appearance.

Wild hair—her smooth blow-dried bob was fast becoming a dim and distant memory—not a trace of make-up and last year's joggers that hung loosely about her slender hips teamed with the cut-off tee shirt that she only normally wore in the gym. Face it, Jude, he's probably seen bag ladies who looked more attractive.

Well, there's news, Jude, you don't meet the fastidious Luca Di Rossi's high standards!

She shifted Amy's weight and hitched her top up over the bare shoulder that had been exposed by the restless baby. It promptly fell off the other shoulder. She began to repeat the process.

'Save it,' a bored I've-seen-it-all-before drawl softly advised. 'I am not my brother.'

The reason he'd chosen to remind her of the one thing she *didn't* need reminding of passed Jude by. A perplexed frown knitting her smooth brow, she gave up on the over-stretched tee shirt. As her eyes collided with his she had several fresh reminders of why she didn't need reminding!

Marco did not make her feel jittery or uncomfortable in her own skin. When he was around her pulse rate behaved beautifully and she could string more than three words together without breaking out in a sweat.

'The helpless act and a little flesh on show will not have me panting!' His eyes narrowed suspiciously.

'Panting…?' she echoed in genuine bewilderment.

'Or did you plant the idea of visiting Marco in the boy's head?'

He was suggesting she would actually…? No, he couldn't be; she must have misheard. Then she saw his contemptuous expression and realised there was no mistake. It took about ten seconds for her temper to reach boiling-point, during which time her complexion went through several dramatic colour changes, settling finally for deathly pale.

'Thanks for that insight, but actually I think I've already got a pretty good idea of what makes you pant.' You and every other man, she thought, watching with satisfaction the bands of dark colour across the twin crests of his high slashing cheekbones.

He scanned her through eyes narrowed to slits. 'And what might that be?' he enquired in a dangerous voice that was as smooth as silk.

'Let me see…' she murmured, raising her eyes to the ceiling in an attitude of deep concentration. 'No, don't tell me,' she begged. 'It's on the tip of my tongue. Blonde hair, long legs…oh, *lots* of flesh on show. Am I warm?' she asked, flashing him an innocent look of enquiry. The icy stare encountered was not encouraging, but Jude found herself in the grip of a strange recklessness and ignored the danger signals. 'Oh, I almost forgot—an ability to treat everything you say as a pearl of wisdom would be a vital ingredient…' Her angry gold-shot eyes clashed with scorching black.

Vile, vile man, she thought, making no attempt to hide her contempt for men like him, the shallow ones who were all gloss and no substance, the ones who could take their pick and inevitably opted for trophy girlfriends.

'Oh, and just for the record I am not helpless!'

'I never imagined you were,' a distracted expression slid into his dark eyes as they slid over rigid outrage. '…but it is a convenient ploy when you require male attention.'

'Why on earth would I require male attention?' she demanded with a contemptuous sniff, before Amy started to whimper again and wriggle.

Luca watched her struggle for a moment. 'That child is tired.'

As he delivered this judgement in a manner that suggested his words were inscribed in stone Amy threw her head back and let out a loud wail. Suddenly everyone's the child-care expert, Jude thought, fast approaching the end of her tether. Except me!

'I'm aware of that,' she snapped. 'If you think you can do better…' she added, glaring at his perfect profile with dislike that seemed to be growing at an alarming rate.

'*Dio mio!*' he ejaculated scornfully as he watched her clumsy attempts to calm the child. 'A moderately well-trained Labrador could do better.'

Jude gave a gasp of outrage and, ready to do battle, threw out her chin, an action that he totally ignored as he looked over her head—an easy thing to do as she barely topped his shoulder. Well, if he was hoping to see a responsible adult he wasn't hoping nearly as much as she was!

'I find it increasingly hard to believe that Joseph's parents have left these children in your care…'

I find it increasingly difficult to believe you are human. Jude gritted her teeth and forced her lips into a smile. The man had brought Joseph safely home—she had to be at least civil, even if he wasn't.

'Well, they have.'

He looked at her face and shook his dark head slowly from side to side in an attitude of insulting disbelief.

'Listen, I really am very grateful to you for returning Joseph.' One of them had to act like a grown-up, she thought, gritting her teeth and thrusting out her hand in an olive-branch fashion.

He looked at her small outstretched hand, but didn't take it. 'Then you had noticed he was missing,' he said in a voice that was all the more deadly for its softness. 'I suppose that's something.'

Her outstretched hand fell to her side as her cheeks burned with angry colour. The caustic, cutting comment was made worse by the fact she couldn't, with a clear conscience, deny it. *As if I needed reminding I'm not fit to look after a goldfish!* Grimly she pushed aside the negative thought. *I'm going to get better at it—even if it kills me!*

'He was only out of my sight for a minute…' Jude cringed inwardly to hear an unattractive whining note of self-justification enter her voice. She buried her face in Amy's soft curls and inhaled the sweet baby smell. 'Hush, darling,' she pleaded raggedly.

Luca gave an exasperated sigh—the quiver in her voice was audible. The girl sounded and looked at the end of her tether. When another child appeared clinging to her leg he gave vent to a hissing sound of exasperation.

This isn't my business, he told himself, glancing at the metal-banded watch on his wrist. The action brought his eyes in line with the innocent, trusting gaze of the little girl peeking out from behind the brunette—her eyes were blue, not brown, but they reminded him very much of Valentina.

CHAPTER THREE

'THIS is an untenable situation,' Luca declared abruptly.

Tell me about it.

The vehemence of his declaration made Sophia, who had crept up behind Jude to get a look at what was going on, grab handfuls of joggers in her chubby hands and duck back behind her aunt, yanking the pants embarrassingly low over Jude's hips in the process.

'I don't know what you're talking about,' Jude said, lifting her head from her efforts to anchor the drawstring waist of her joggers before it revealed more than it already had.

She discovered that his dark gaze was fixed on the expanse of her flat stomach and midriff. Something electrifying and scary rushed through her body. Her bare skin tingled as if he had touched her.

'Admiring my appendix scar?'

If she'd thought to discompose him, Jude was disappointed. However, her own composure fled when the heavy screen of dark lashes lifted, revealing the glitter of dark eyes beneath.

There was nothing covert about the smouldering sexual appraisal. The breath snagged in her throat as she tried to swallow past the occlusion in her dry throat. She wrenched her eyes from his, horribly conscious of the heavy dragging sensation low in her belly and her pinched nipples burning as they rubbed against her tight, constricting top.

Head bent, she hastily yanked the joggers around her waist and cinched the cord tight. She didn't look up until the dizziness that had made her head spin had lessened. Jude was furious with her body for betraying her this way. Anyone would think a man had never looked at her before!

'I'm sorry to have taken so much of your time.' Her cold words were as clear an invitation for him to leave as you could get without saying get lost.

'Just how many children are you meant to be looking after?' he demanded, striding decisively into the room. 'Are there any more hiding anywhere?'

Jude clenched her teeth as he stepped past her. Obviously she'd been too subtle. Maybe she should have stuck with get lost.

As his dark eyes scanned the untidy room she repressed a ridiculous impulse to apologise for the mess.

'Mr Di Rossi, I'm really very grateful to you for returning Joseph safe and sound but—'

He cut in without even looking at her. 'You have the telephone number of the children's parents?'

The unexpected question hit her like a physical blow. 'No.'

It was the sharp inhalation and not the brief reply that followed that brought his attention zeroing back to her face. A perplexed frown drew his dark brows together as he encountered the inexplicable shimmer of unshed tears in her wide, luminous eyes. Her soft lips definitely trembled before she caught her full lower lip between her teeth.

'What sort of parents would not leave a contact number?'

'You leave them alone!' she snapped.

Luca looked from her flushed face to the small white-knuckled fist she had pressed to her mouth. 'I am not leaving anyone alone until I have satisfied myself that these children are safe.'

'Of course they're safe.'

His dark glance slid significantly to Joseph, who was playing with his sister at the opposite end of the room, and Jude flushed. He smiled—it was not a nice smile. She hit back instinctively.

'At least I don't go around bashing—' The silence that followed her abbreviated accusation simply simmered with tension.

One dark brow lifted as he replied in a slow, measured, conversational tone. 'You were saying…?' Like black ice, his stunning eyes rested unblinkingly on her burning face. Jude, already slightly ashamed of her below-the-belt jibe, squirmed.

'Sensitive subject?' she threw back recklessly.

It was nothing short of amazing, she reflected, unable to tear her eyes from his extraordinary face, that such extremes of emotions could be conveyed with little more than a quiver of a nostril and a twitch of an eyebrow. Although he had done nothing more than this, it was pretty clear that Luca Di Rossi was in the grip of *extremely* extreme emotion at that moment.

'As someone who clearly believes I am indeed a man who vents his anger on anyone who can't hit back, you must be hoping it isn't a sensitive subject,' he observed softly.

He's right, she thought. I'm standing in the presence of just about the most physically intimidating male I have ever met, who, just to make life interesting, has a well-rumoured inability to control his temper, and I'm winding him up. Either I'm very stupid or I don't believe the stories.

The former was debatable, but, rather to her own surprise, Jude found that the latter was true. Luca Di Rossi might well be The World's Most Notorious Playboy, but she didn't believe for one minute he went around hitting women—he might wish he could right now, but he didn't.

'What makes you think I can't hit back?'

His look of amused condescension made her wish she'd attended more than two of the judo classes she'd begun with such enthusiasm. I would most likely be a black belt at least by now—the man did say I showed promise. Then, she thought viciously, I could wipe that smile right off his face. For a moment she allowed herself to wistfully visualise herself victoriously astride his prone body, completely at her mercy—*completely*!

Jude blinked and gave her head a tiny shake as her imagination, a little overexcited by the image, began to embellish the scene dangerously. Clearing her throat, she turned her attention to the real thing—he wasn't at her mercy. He had probably never been at anyone's mercy in his life; he was your original in-control man.

'You're not going to go away, are you?' she said, a note of dull resignation in her voice.

'Not until I am sure there is someone capable to take care of these children.'

'Do you *always* get what you want?'

'Eventually,' he admitted factually. 'There is actually nothing more I would like to do than walk out of that door,' he added with an expressive shrug of his shoulders. 'However, I feel it is my duty under the circumstances to inform these children's parents that they have left them in the care of someone who is clearly not up to the task,' he explained formally.

That's what I've been trying to tell everyone. The irony of finally finding someone who agreed with her brought a bitter smile to Jude's lips.

'Duty?'

His lip curled contemptuously. 'A foreign concept to you?'

You pompous…prig. A man who dumped girlfriends the way other men changed their socks knew a lot about duty. 'I'm familiar with it,' she admitted. 'I'm just surprised someone like you is.'

He sucked in his breath nosily and fixed her with a cold and unforgiving knife-edged stare. 'I don't know what these people expect, leaving their children in the care of an irresponsible teenager.'

Jude was so absorbed with scoring points in the battle of insults that the significance of what he'd said didn't sink in for several seconds. She scanned his face incredulously. He was serious—he actually thought she was a teenage babysitter! The incredulous laugh that was wrenched from her throat brought his dark, frowning disapproval.

Considering that she felt as though she'd aged twenty years over the past four weeks, it was almost flattering—*almost*!

'I'm not the babysitter,' she stated, placing Amy on the floor. The toddler crawled a couple of feet before grabbing a coffee-table to haul herself to her feet. 'Neither,' she added, flexing her wrist to ease the ache where she'd been carrying the baby, 'am I a teenager.'

Jude didn't have opportunity to savour him looking nonplussed by her response as the twins chose that precise moment to begin to squabble over a toy.

'Can you do nothing about this racket?' Luca demanded, raising his voice above the din.

'Children make noise; it's what they do.' On this score at least she felt qualified to give an opinion. It was actually something of a confidence boost to encounter someone who knew *less* about the practicalities of child care than she did. 'And actually,' honesty impelled her to add, 'it's pointless me trying to make them stop—they won't listen to me.'

He responded to her frank admission by snorting something in rapid Italian, which, if the look of unqualified contempt that accompanied it was any indicator, was not complimentary!

'Fine—you think you can do better,' she choked, 'feel free!'

To judge by their expressions the children were just as amazed as she was to see the authoritative figure of Luca Di Rossi take up her challenge. A stunned silence fell as he bent over and calmly confiscated the item they were fighting over.

'If you are unable to share, perhaps it is better that I keep this,' he told them repressively.

'But...'

Joseph's half-hearted protest was stilled by a single look from the tall man. Even whilst she resented the way he was usurping her role, Jude secretly envied his ability to inspire unquestioning obedience in the children.

'Do you have a box for these toys?' Two blond heads gave an affirmative nod. 'Then I suggest you put them in it before someone breaks their neck.'

'You can't speak to the children like that,' she hissed, catching his arm.

His eyes touched the hand she had laid on his arm to get his attention before shifting to her face. 'Like what?'

'So harshly,' she explained, rubbing her palm against her thigh. 'They're...they've had a lot of...upset in their lives lately—they need tender loving care, not being bawled at by a big bully.' She could no longer resist sliding a furtive peek at his upper arm; her stomach dipped as she recalled how hard it had felt. Even more inexplicable had been the strange reluctance she had felt to remove her hand.

'I was not harsh,' he denied. 'I was firm, and children need to know the boundaries; it makes them feel secure. This is *especially* important during times of upheaval—children need continuity.'

Jude stared at him in frustration. She could hardly denounce what he was saying when she had a string of letters after her name that said *she* was the one who ought to be saying it. It was after all pretty basic stuff, but as she'd discovered the gap between theory and practice was pretty big, especially when you were thinking with your heart not your head.

She pushed an unsteady hand through her hair. I'm just too involved to be objective, she concluded unhappily.

'You didn't have to be so…so brutal,' she denounced stubbornly.

One eloquent brow lifted. He inclined his head towards the children. 'Do they look crushed or traumatised?'

Jude normally had no problem with admitting when she was wrong, but on this occasion— 'You can't always tell with children.'

The look he directed at her made Jude flush and turn away.

It would be very easy to hate someone who made it look so easy, she thought, watching the twins doing as he had instructed and acting as though it was an enormous treat. It didn't help knowing full well that if *she* had suggested they pick up their toys they would have given her an exhaustive argument before ignoring her.

Jude didn't know what was more difficult to believe: their co-operative behaviour or the inescapable fact that The World's Most Notorious Playboy knew about children. He was the very last man in the world she would have had down as being comfortable with children.

'If this baby has a cot,' he said, switching his attention to Amy, 'I suggest you put her in it.'

And the hell of it is, Jude thought as she tucked Amy in, I did exactly what I was told. It was mortifying.

To compensate for her meek compliance Jude returned to the living room with a combative tilt to her chin and a determined gleam in her eyes. She was going to get rid of Mr Child Expert Di Rossi after she had told him exactly what she thought of him. It was one thing for her to say that she was not up to the job, it was quite another for a perfect stranger to point it out!

He looked up as she entered. The room, she immediately noticed, was already looking less like a disaster area and the twins were contentedly playing like model children in a corner.

Joseph smiled as he caught sight of her. 'Aunty Jude, do they have phones in heaven?'

Jude froze, aghast at this evidence their low-voiced conversation had been overheard. 'No, darling, I'm afraid they don't. Mr Di Rossi can't call heaven,' she said huskily.

Joseph gave a sigh that broke her heart and returned to his quiet game.

'Would you two like to go and play on the computer for half an hour?' she asked, a tell-tale quiver in her painfully bright voice.

The twins responded eagerly to the offer and ran off to the study, which was a rather grand name for something that was little more than a cupboard. As they slammed the door behind them Jude released a deep sigh and covered her face with her hands.

Since the funeral she'd imagined that she'd wake up one morning and find it had all been a bad dream. The little boy's question had brought it home; she was living the bad dream and they weren't coming home—ever!

The brutal pain of loss was physical as she made herself think of them in the past tense. David and Sam had been the original odd couple. Many had shaken their heads and said it would never last when they'd married, but they'd proved the critics wrong.

It had been a classic case of opposites attracting. Her brother had been to patience what his wife had been to organisation. Ironically David, with his obsessive need for punctuality, had got married to a woman who'd been late for everything.

Jude could remember asking her sister-in-law once if she didn't mind always putting her own needs last.

'I've never been this happy in my life,' Sam had replied simply. 'You just wait until it happens to you, Jude, and you'll see what I mean.'

'Oh, it's not going to happen to me,' Jude had replied confidently. 'I'm never going to give up my freedom to be at the beck and call of some man, and I'm just not the maternal type.'

Sam had just laughed and said, 'We'll see.' In that enigmatic, irritating way that married people did with singles.

Jude's opinion of marriage and motherhood hadn't changed, but after a month of trying to fill her sister-in-law's shoes she was beginning to appreciate just how hard it was to be even a mediocre mother, let alone a brilliant one as Sam had been.

'I didn't realise they were listening to us.'

Luca looked at the down-bent head of the young woman and his severe expression softened. 'Children have a habit of hearing more than you imagine,' he told her with the voice of experience. 'Both parents?' he added abruptly.

With a shuddering sigh Jude lowered her hands. 'Yes, both,' she confirmed bleakly. 'It was a car accident last month.'

'Last month? *Madre di Dio!* What a tragedy.' His eyes went to the door behind which the children's laughter could be heard. 'Why didn't you simply tell me the children's parents were dead?'

Jude shook her head. 'I don't know.'

A hiss of exasperation escaped his clenched teeth at her weak reply. 'And this is you? Dr Judith Lucas…?'

Jude saw for the first time that he was holding a paperback copy of her book. The photo on the flyleaf was turned to her and he appeared to be scanning the bio on the inner page.

'Yes,' she admitted. Not much point denying it; the photo was not a good likeness but it was still recognisably her, even if the powers that be had decided to opt for a sexy look as opposed to studious.

'*You* wrote a book on child care?' Luca drawled, closing the book and running his index finger down the spine before replacing the book on the shelf he had removed it from. His eyes touched her face and Jude nodded. 'And people *read* it?'

She flushed at the heavily satiric note in his voice. 'I've had a lot of letters from parents who found it very useful,' she gritted defiantly.

'Is that so?'

'Are you calling me a liar?'

'I was merely thinking that if this is such a good book it might be a good idea if you read it yourself.' His smooth, hateful drawl brought a flush to her cheeks. 'I'm sure you offered your services to the children's guardian from the best motives,' he conceded stiffly, 'but it was hardly prudent considering—'

'Considering what?' Conscious that her raised voice might be able to be heard in the next room, Jude made an effort to moderate her tone. But it was hard to be moderate when you were talking to a man who had a first-class honours degree in patronising, a man who insulted you every time he opened his mouth and treated you as if you were a total fool. 'That I'm totally clueless?' she hissed.

'The facts speak for themselves,' he told her bluntly. 'I'm sure you're just great chairing a group therapy session.' Though frankly he couldn't see it. 'But you don't know the first thing about children…'

His condescension grated on her almost as much as his accuracy. 'I don't actually practice, I lecture at the university and I never claimed that I had hands-on experience,' she snapped.

'Some things are taken as read. You writing a book on child care is like a virgin writing a sex manual. You're not one of those too, are you?'

'Of course not, don't be stupid!'

He shot her a strange look. 'I wasn't actually being serious.'

Jude didn't like his calculating expression. 'I know that...' she retorted quickly.

After all, you couldn't tell by *looking* at a person, and the surest way to make people suspect was to start acting weird every time someone said virgin.

'What exactly is your relationship to the children? I'm assuming that Aunty is a courtesy title?'

'No, it isn't. David, their father, was my brother.'

A nerve beside his expressive mouth jumped; you could almost see his brain making the necessary links and coming up with the unlikely conclusion. '*You* are their guardian?'

Dark eyes scanned her face, interpreting the over-prominent cheekbones, the lines of strain around her mouth and the violet bruises beneath her eyes in the light of this astounding information. 'This cannot be.'

'Why, because *you* say so?' His face darkened with displeasure at her sarcastic jibe. *Tough*, Jude thought, her jaw tightening. In some corner of her mind, where a professionally trained part of herself lurked, she knew that she was focusing all her pent-up frustration and aggression on him—but what the hell? He looked big enough to take it!

'*Because*,' he contradicted in a driven voice, 'I think it's a formula for disaster to leave children in the care of someone who will probably reach adolescence at the same time as them. I suppose you thought it was very amusing to deceive me?'

It was the extraordinary addition rather than the insult that preceded it that made Jude's eyes fly open. How did he have the barefaced cheek to say that? This man was totally unbelievable.

'What are you on?' she quivered. 'I hate to be the one to break this to you but some people have more important things on their mind than making you look silly. I didn't do any deceiving!' she yelled. 'It was you, you couldn't wait to jump to conclusions,' she accused—even if, barring the teenage thing, they were essentially correct.

'What was I meant to think?' Luca demanded. 'You have no control over the children in your care. Your manner, your dress is not that of a woman.' His furious eyes flicked scornfully over her rigid figure. 'Everything about you suggests adolescence and immaturity. If it was not your intention to deceive then I must conclude that you have a lot of growing up to do,' he delivered scornfully.

As she listened to this ruthless character assessment his features swam out of focus as hot, angry tears of humiliation filled her eyes. Jude pressed one clenched fist against her mouth before she had enough control of her temper to speak. It was not in her nature to take such treatment lying down.

Luca caught the shimmer of tears in the beautiful eyes before she turned her head away. The fine quiver of muscles just below the surface in her pale throat suggested she was fighting for control.

In business dealings he never allowed the opposition to provoke him into using unconsidered language; this was a philosophy that he carried through to his personal life. As the heat of anger dissipated Luca became dismayed by his failure to follow his own golden rule. As infuriating as he found her sharp-tongued antagonism and total lack of respect, he found the young woman's dejected demeanour and bowed head infinitely harder to endure.

He admired spirit and would no more have wanted to extinguish the characteristic in this infuriating female than he would have crushed the spirit of the fine Arabian horses he bred on the Umbrian estate where he spent most of his leisure time.

Luca admired spirit.

The moment her head lifted he realised his lament for her fire and spirit had been premature.

'If we're going to get into character analysis I'd say a man over thirty who mentally strips a woman he thinks is a teenager stands some examination!'

'Dio!'

The dark stain of colour that accentuated his cheekbones was proof her jibe had found its mark. A muscle clenched in his lean cheek as he looked down at her from his superior height as if she were a sub species not fit to grovel at his feet.

'Men look, it is their nature,' he framed with a shrug.

Jude got the impression, despite his cool contention, her remark had really got to him. 'Well, it's not my nature to stand there and take it.'

'Oh, was that not the reaction you wanted?' he returned, sounding surprised.

Now wasn't that just like a man to blame the woman? 'Sure, I just *love* being drooled over by some oversexed, lecherous pig! It sets me up beautifully for the rest of the day.'

He froze and looked at her as if he couldn't believe what she had said. His entire body was rigid with a combination of outrage and disbelief.

'Your problem is you're just not *man* enough to admit you're in the wrong.' A person would be excused for thinking I *wanted* to see him flip. Whatever his expression he was beautiful, but wanting to strangle her really gave him an extra edge, she admitted, suppressing a little shiver of excitement as she covertly admired the strong lines of his impassioned face.

'Dio!' His nostrils flared as he inhaled deeply, fighting an uphill battle to contain his feelings. 'Calling a man's masculinity into question is a dangerous tactic, Dr Lucas…'

'Oh, spare me the macho demonstrations. Besides, if you can't take a few home truths you shouldn't have been so free with your opinions.' It was totally irrational and it wasn't as if she suffered from low self-esteem or anything, but his words had hurt—not that she had any intention of letting him see that.

He looked at her, no trace of comprehension on his drop-dead gorgeous features.

'You felt at liberty to insult me,' she reminded him. He continued to look blank. 'You said I wasn't a woman.' To her horror Jude was unable to control the noisy sob that rose convulsively in her throat, then another and another. They shook her slender frame, gathering force with each successive one.

'Are you crying?'

Not here, not now, *please*!

'What does it look like I'm doing?'

Even as she was in the process of delivering her acid retort Luca could almost hear the sound of her control snapping. He blamed himself for being too distracted to register that she had been on the brink of this breakdown. All the signs had been there. He was naturally sympathetic to her loss, but he had enough problems of his own without getting caught up in someone else's trauma.

'You said I'm hopeless with children,' she began in a low, impassioned voice, 'and you're right!' she declared with a bitter laugh. 'I am, I'm a total, complete failure. If it hadn't been for you goodness knows what would have happened to Joseph…' She turned horror-drenched eyes to him.

'There is absolutely no point going down the road of what-if scenarios. The point is Joseph is well and safe.'

Jude shook her head, refusing to be comforted. 'Despite me, not because of me. But I'm all they've got, you see, and I've got to g…get it right!' she cried, her voice rising to a teary crescendo of seismic self-pity.

The sound made Luca, who was standing stock-still, wince.

Jude wiped her hands across her damp face and tried to get her breath, which was emerging as a series of uneven gulps.

'I never cry,' she explained just before she released another shocking wail.

She never lost sight of the fact that she was going to regret this display, but this knowledge had no power to stem the unbridled misery that seeped out of her. For so long she had been unable to cry and now she couldn't stop. *What terrible timing I have!*

Luca glanced towards the closed door behind which the loud noises of a computer game could be heard as the slender, hunched figure gave way once more to sobs.

'I'm terrible at all this, you know!' *What am I saying? Of course he knows.* 'And,' she wailed, lifting her tragic red-rimmed eyes to his and delivering a bitter pronouncement, 'I'll never have sex again! It's not funny,' she yelled when he callously smiled.

'Per amor di Dio!' Luca muttered softly under his breath as, sobbing helplessly, she pulled a tissue from her sleeve and blew her nose noisily. 'Come here,' he instructed, a note of exasperation in his deep voice.

There was no resistance in the pliant body he drew against his. She felt cold, incredibly fragile and strangely the essence of everything that was female. A deep sigh vibrated through her slender frame as he smoothed down her hair in a distracted fashion. She burrowed into him with a soft, trusting sigh and Luca, who could have identified any number of expensive perfumes, found himself unable to place the disturbing scent that filled his nostrils.

They stood that way for some time. Luca felt the exact moment she stopped reacting like a hurt animal seeking comfort and became aware of where she was and who he was—the enemy. Her body jackknifed away from him.

Jude pushed her hair from her face and raised aghast eyes to his. 'I don't know why that happened.' She blinked in a bewildered fashion.

'Perhaps because you haven't let it happen before.'

He might have a point, she admitted, blotting the tear stains with the back of her hand. Luca seemed to be taking being cried all over by a hysterical woman rather better than she would have imagined, she thought, casting a wary glance at his criminally handsome face.

Maybe this sort of stuff happened to him a lot, women flinging themselves on his manly chest? A more worrying thought was him thinking she went around doing this sort of thing on a regular basis!

'Maybe, but I'm really sorry about subjecting you to that.' She sniffed. She sensed she was going to be even sorrier at some stage now that she knew what it felt like to be in his arms.

'Why do the English feel the need to apologise for displays of emotion?' he wondered drily. 'If you let go of your emotions once in a while people like you might be out of a job.'

His ironic words passed over her head. 'Pardon?' She found it hard to look at him and not recall how hard his body had been or how good it had felt—so don't look at him, idiot! She inhaled and discovered the warm, musky male scent of him was still in her nostrils. She lowered her eyes quickly.

Luca placed a finger under her chin and firmly tilted her face upwards. He scanned her tear-stained face critically. 'When did you last have any sleep?' he demanded.

'I'm fine.' He was looking at her much the way he had Joseph when he'd considered defying him. There was nothing *remotely* childlike about the way she was feeling.

'I am not considered to be a patient man.'

This drew a weak laugh from her. 'Now there's a surprise.'

'When?'

She frowned in concentration. 'I think I had a couple of hours last night.'

'You know, the world might look less bleak if you had a decent night's sleep. Is there no one who could help you out with the children to let you get some sleep? Your mother, maybe?'

This suggestion produced a bitter laugh. It had been David who had pointed out the obvious to her when they'd been in their teens.

'Of course Mum's keen on us being self-reliant, Judy. It makes life easier for her if we're not expecting to be bailed out of trouble every five minutes.' David had developed a philosophical attitude to their mother's brutal sink-or-swim approach earlier than she had.

'My mother has a meeting.' Could I sound more bitter and twisted?

'That sounds like an unresolved issue—is that the correct psycho-babble speak?'

'It works,' she agreed.

'In that case I won't go there.'

'That's a pretty good call.'

'As for having sex, I do not think you should totally give up on that, *cara*.'

Jude froze at the sex bit; by the time he'd completed his sentence her respiratory muscles had stopped working. For a little while there she'd convinced herself she either hadn't said what she thought she had, or he hadn't heard it. It hardly seemed possible you could be this embarrassed and not die!

'Easy for you to say,' she croaked.

Jude's eyes widened with alarm as he framed her face between his hands, his thumb stroking the delicate but firm line of her jaw as he studied her. Jude trembled, totally mesmerised by the hungry expression that slid into his dark eyes. Luca's breathing quickened as he watched the pupils of her eyes dilate.

When his hands abruptly fell away Jude was left with knees of cotton wool and a terrible sense of anticlimax.

'Trust me on this one,' he suggested in a strangely grim manner.

CHAPTER FOUR

JUDE never knew where she got the nerve and plain reckless insanity to do what she did next.

Conceivably some residual effects of Luca's touch had something to do with it, or maybe it was the depressing vision of the enforced celibacy of her future she saw stretching before her that made her a little crazy.

At least this way I'll have something to remember.

Boldly she took hold of Luca's dark head. As her fingers sank into the sleek, glossy pelt that covered his head she realised that she'd actually been wondering what this would feel like from the moment she'd opened the door and found him standing there.

As she dragged him down to her level she stretched upwards on tiptoe until their faces were almost level. In the nanosecond just before she placed her lips against his she looked directly into his eyes; what she saw smouldering in his gave her the courage to take the last step.

After all the build-up it was a bit of an anticlimax. Almost before she even started kissing him a persistent voice in her head put a damper on things by saying, You thought this was a good idea because…?

It was probably just as well because actually things weren't going well; kissing someone who was taking no active part was no more fun than she remembered kissing the back of her hand to practise her technique had been when she was twelve.

She began to pull back, she *would have* pulled back had not Luca suddenly murmured something harsh and uneven against her mouth in his native tongue. Out of nowhere the chemistry materialised; the air around crackled with the energy looking for an outlet.

Her face was framed between his big hands as she stood there rigid, her enormous eyes shadowy smudges in her pale face, feeling his tongue trace the outline of her lips.

'Oh, my God!' Her insides melted. She made a final total protest before giving into the heat coursing through her veins. 'This isn't a good idea.'

'You thought it was a minute ago,' Luca, whose thoughts had also been running very much along those lines, rebuked her throatily.

'I've stopped thinking.' It was true—gone was the inhibiting voice-over she had never been able to silence before when she'd been kissed. It had always been as if part of her had remained separate from what had been happening. *'That's* never happened before.'

He laughed at her husky confidence, but it didn't lessen the tension she felt emanating from his big body as he turned her face between his hands, examining her flushed features in a manner that suggested compulsion rather than curiosity.

'Maybe you should stop talking too,' he observed, sliding his tongue between her invitingly parted lips.

At the first stabbing incursion a wave of extreme lethargy rolled over Jude, and as the air was snatched from her lungs in one breathy gasp she went totally limp.

Instead of catching her Luca controlled her stumble, allowing the impetus to take them both the several feet to the wall.

A disorientated Jude found herself standing with her back pressed against the wall, her hands pinioned either side of her head. She gasped and stopped moving; the friction created as her breasts pressed against Luca's chest sent darts of painful pleasure through her body.

'This isn't happening!'

'You're in denial, Doctor,' he diagnosed, transferring both her hands to one of his and using his freed hand to caress her face.

I'm in deep trouble, she thought, running the tip of her tongue across her swollen, tender lips as his hand lightly skimmed across her middle, then slid more firmly down her thigh.

'*Dio, cara*, kiss me!' he instructed, releasing her hands and taking a step back from her.

Her response to the sound of his voice was so extreme she didn't want to think about what would happen if he did more than talk. Of course, inevitably she *did* think about it. Jude had no control over the low feral moan that issued from deep in her throat as she wound her arms around his neck. Strong arms circled her waist as he effortlessly lifted her face up to his level.

Their lips touched and there simply wasn't anything else. His competence in the kissing department was only to be expected, but it was the raw desperation that laced his expertise that enchanted her.

When they finally broke apart they were both panting as their eyes reconnected. The need stamped on his dark, tense features excited her almost beyond endurance.

She hadn't known that wanting someone could physically hurt.

Luca's eyes had followed every flicker of emotion across her expressive face. It was fascinating to watch; he had never seen anyone whose emotions were so close to the surface. Her ability to respond and react as though everything she was experiencing was a first-time thing was amazing.

As her eyelashes began to settle protectively against waxily pale cheeks he shook his head. 'No, I want to see your face.' As her chin lifted he pressed the lower half of his body to hers until their bodies were sealed thigh to thigh.

Jude's eyes flew open to their fullest extent as she felt the brazen pressure of his erection grind into the softness of her lower belly. His eyes burned into hers so hot she felt the prickle of tears sting the back of her eyelids. Everything about him was hot and she just wanted to be part of that heat, to lose herself in it and him. It never even occurred to her to pull back in protest; instead, back arched, she pressed herself into his heat and hardness, striving to seal their bodies even more intimately together.

He kissed her again and again, deep, searing kisses, as though he couldn't get enough of her. It took Jude longer to respond to the sound of the door opening than Luca.

When the children ran into the room Jude was banging the TV remote on her thigh, babbling in a high-pitched voice, 'It must need new batteries and I really wanted to watch that documentary.'

Luca adjusted his jacket and smoothed down his tousled hair, no trace of the paralysing embarrassment she was feeling evident in his relaxed manner. 'Which documentary would that be?'

Jude's reproachful gaze flickered to his face.

Oh, God, how could I?

'I…I forget.'

'Aunty Jude, have you been crying?' Joseph's voice shattered the tense atmosphere.

With a bright smile on her face, Jude turned to the little boy. 'No, of course not, darling.' But she felt like it now. Her entire body burned with humiliation. It was a nightmare—

the one where you were in the supermarket when you realised you were only wearing your undies, and they weren't the nice glamorous ones but the ones that had seen too many wash cycles.

She couldn't look at him, but she was overpoweringly conscious of his scrutiny. Right from the off her reaction to him had been pretty schizophrenic, but to kiss him…? God, it had gone way beyond kissing.

'She *was* crying before cos you were lost,' Sophia announced.

'I wasn't lost,' Joseph denied indignantly. 'I knew exactly where I was. I have Daddy's sense of direction,' he explained proudly.

He sounded so like his father that Jude could hardly keep the tears in check. 'That,' she said in a shaking voice, 'is as maybe, but you must never, *ever* go anywhere without asking me first. Is that understood?'

To Jude's immense frustration the little boy glanced almost imperceptibly to the masculine figure beside her before coming up with a suitably contrite, 'Yes, Aunty Jude.'

All she needed was for Joseph, starved of a male role model, to decide to put Luca in that part. It was a very worrying development, because Mr Di Rossi was going to disappear off their horizon for ever any second now.

'Now I think we should all say a big thank-you to Mr Di Rossi,' she said brightly. What should I thank him for? Turning me into a sex-starved idiot, maybe? 'Especially you, Joseph, for being such a bother.'

'I wasn't a bother, was I, Luca? You like me, don't you?' he suggested with a guileless smile.

'And me,' his twin piped up, giving her brother a shove.

'You're both revolting.'

To Jude's total amazement this growled response appeared to delight the children, who both began to giggle helplessly.

'See, Aunty Jude, he likes us,' Joseph told her complacently.

Jude's eyes suddenly filled. She turned away, but not before Luca had seen the shimmer. A little bit of hero worship was harmless, but it concerned her that they were so hungry for love.

Maybe it's not *their* hunger for love you're worried about?

'Of course he likes you.' She smiled mechanically as memories of her wanton behaviour flashed kaleidoscope-fashion before her eyes.

'Can Luca stay for tea?'

'I'm afraid that isn't possible, children.'

Jude hated to see their little faces fall, but in the long run it was better for them not to nurse false hopes.

'Mr Di Rossi is a very busy man.'

Luca squatted down to child height. 'Perhaps one day you could come and have tea with me at my house in the country. I have a little girl who is only a little older than you two.'

'Wow, can we, Aunty Jude?'

'We'll see.'

Once she had reached the front door with Luca she allowed her anger to boil over. With a quick glance over her shoulder, she followed him into the corridor, leaving the door behind her ajar so that she could hear should the children need her.

Her hair lashed across her face as she spun around, eyes blazing, to face him. 'How dare you fob the children off with false promises?' she demanded in a furious whisper. 'It was cruel and unnecessary, but I don't suppose you thought beyond getting away without a fuss and remaining the nice guy,' she sneered, pausing to catch her breath.

'Well, congratulations, they think you're a hero, but it's me who will see their faces when they don't get an invite to tea.' She rubbed her nose vigorously with the back of her hand as her feelings threatened to overcome her. 'You can walk away and never think of them again—' she frowned to hear the quivery note in her voice '—but *I'm* the one who will have to come up with an explanation,' she finished with breathless resentment.

Luca appeared to listen attentively but remained frustratingly unmoved by her recriminations. For several moments he just stood scanning her angry, tear-stained features with an enigmatic expression.

'What?' she demanded querulously when he just carried on staring.

'You don't wish me to walk away? Is that the problem here?'

Jude flushed at the sly insinuation in his amused voice. 'You walking away is the *solution*. You can vanish in a puff of blue smoke for all I care.'

This childish declaration brought a sudden grin of quite devastating charm to his lean face. 'You know, I suddenly see the family resemblance. I think,' he decided, after peering at her through thoughtfully narrowed eyes, 'that it's the pout.'

'I do not pout!' she denied crossly. Then she noticed his eyes were still fixed on her lips and he wasn't smiling. Her sensitive stomach flipped and she rushed into speech to fill the dangerous silence developing. 'The problem is you lying to the children without thinking of the consequences. I suppose the daughter doesn't exist either.'

'She does and her name is Valentina.'

'Oh!'

'And the only time I have not considered the consequences of my actions was when I kissed you.'

So fine, he regretted kissing her—she could live with that. 'Forget it,' she suggested casually. 'I have. It was nothing.'

'It was many things, but we both know *nothing* is not one of them.'

'So what did you have in mind? Disgusting? Revolting?

Well, let me tell you, for someone who didn't like it you seemed to be putting a lot of effort into it at the time!'

'Does frustration always make you this cranky?'

'Frustration?'

'That's the risk you take when you start something you can't finish.'

His meaning finally hit her. 'Good God, there was never any chance of…me…' She shook her head vigorously. 'None whatsoever!' she insisted.

His dark, implacable eyes drilled into her. 'You wanted me.'

More than I've ever wanted anything in my life.

'If we hadn't been interrupted we'd have ended up in bed, or, more realistically, on that nice rug. We wouldn't have made it as far as the bedroom.'

The erotic image his soft, insidious words conjured was so vivid that for a moment she could almost hear the hoarse pleas emerging from her mouth! She literally shook herself to expel the wanton images crowding into her brain.

'You're crude and disgusting!' she choked, pressing her trembling hands to her flaming cheeks.

His eyes brushed her face. 'And you are the most amazingly passionate woman I have ever met. It was like holding a flame in my arms.'

Me?

'We both know what I'm saying is so.'

Stubbornly she shook her head.

'And I did not lie to the children—I would like them to visit. We've just moved over from Italy and Valentina has no friends yet. It would be good for her to meet children near her own age. I could show you our new house—it is an old vicarage in the countryside. It had nine bedrooms—the housekeeper seems obsessed with keeping all those beds…?' He spread his hands in a very Latin gesture of appeal.

'Aired?'

'Thank you. I understand that sleeping in them is the best method of doing this. We could use them on a rotational basis.'

'I don't want to see your house, I don't want to sleep in your beds and I don't want to see you.'

'You would have me break my promise to the children?' he asked.

Jude literally ground her teeth in frustration. 'I would have you get lost,' she hissed ungrammatically. 'I don't want to sleep with you.'

'Don't you believe in fate? I do,' he revealed. 'And I think you and I are fated to be lovers.'

Luca looked out over the incredible vista of the city and didn't see a thing as he picked up the phone and dialled.

'Get me everything you can on a Judith Lucas—she lives in this building. *Dr* Lucas—she's a psychologist.'

'Finally getting therapy, are you? Good move. Listen, Luca, I know you pay me well, mate, but the private detective stuff really isn't in my remit.'

'I need someone I trust, Tom.'

There was a pause the other end. 'This isn't about what we were talking about earlier, is it?' There was a troubled note in the lawyer's voice.

'I think she might be my future wife,' Luca confirmed simply.

'You can't marry a total stranger, Luca.'

'Have you never heard of fate, my friend?'

'Fate! Have you been drinking, Luca?'

With a smile Luca poured a measure of brandy into a glass. 'Oh and, Tom, I'd like to know if she's slept with my brother.'

There was an even longer pause. 'And if she has would that make a difference?'

'Only to my tactics, not my intentions.'

'Remind me never to own anything you want, Luca,' the other man said wryly.

Luca replaced the receiver and took a swallow of the golden liquid, savouring the taste as it slid over his tongue.

CHAPTER FIVE

'CAN I have a kite?' the little boy asked wistfully, watching a child in the distance who was being taught the art of kite-flying by her father.

The response she'd always sworn as a child that she was never, ever going to say to *her* children sprang automatically to Jude's lips. 'Maybe.'

'Dad said I could have a kite.'

Jude bit her lip. 'I said we'll see, Joseph,' she said huskily. 'Now keep up, please, there's a good boy.'

'That's Luca!' Sophia suddenly shouted as she pointed to the path a little farther ahead.

'Luca! Luca!' Oblivious to Jude's remonstration not to run ahead, they both ran off.

Being a responsible adult meant she couldn't obey her own instincts, which were telling her to run too—in the opposite direction. Taking a deep breath and hoping that her knees would not fold under her at an inappropriate moment, she was left with no choice but to follow, but at a more sedate pace dictated by the buggy she was pushing.

It was possible to disguise the fact she was about two heartbeats away from total panic by the time she reached the group with a relaxed and confident smile. It was less easy to disguise the fact she could hardly breathe.

There was another man with Luca and a little girl who looked to be around seven or eight.

Pinning her glassy gaze at some point over Luca's shoulder, she hoped he'd put her raised colour down to her recent exertion, and *not* her inability to look at him and not imagine him wearing nothing at all! She let her stiff smile embrace all three, aiming for polite but distant.

The effort made beads of sweat break out across her upper lip. Moistening her dry lips with the tip of her tongue, she tucked her resilient curls behind her ears. Her racing heart was trying to batter its way out of her chest.

Her eyes skimmed over his tall, distinctive figure without focusing. It had taken her a sleepless night to reach an explanation she could live with—namely what she had felt and *done*, could all be attributed to her overwrought condition. A condition exacerbated by sleep deprivation, which everyone knew could make a person act peculiar.

A doctorate and all I can come up with is *peculiar*! If this whole scenario weren't so horrifying she'd have laughed.

'Dr Lucas…' Luca greeted her with his hand outstretched. One dark brow took on a satiric slant when she didn't make any effort to take his extended hand, but he didn't comment.

Touching him voluntarily was totally out of the question. A wave of heat washed over her as she looked at him—if she'd been overreacting last night, she still was.

Like her he was casually dressed, in a white tee shirt and black jeans, but, unlike her own faded denims that because of her recent weight loss fitted loosely over her hips, his clung lovingly to the well-developed lines of his long thighs.

She was suddenly neck-deep in a confused mess of high-octane excitement, sexual longing and fear.

'What a pleasant surprise.'

Speak for yourself.

Their eyes touched and she discovered he was lying. He'd known she was going to be here; maybe he'd even followed her. Oh, God! Now I think rich and powerful men are following me—I really have lost it!

Despite the fact she knew it made no sense, her gut feeling this was no accidental meeting persisted. Maybe the kiss had kept him awake all night too. Jude, who didn't number vanity amongst her faults, gave a self-derisive little grimace. He'd probably forgotten she existed before he'd returned to the luxury of his own apartment.

'Can I introduce my friend Carlo?'

Jude's eyes widened fractionally as she focused on the older man. The thick-set figure, who was almost as broad as he was tall, smiled. The action pulled at the puckered scar that ran from one corner of his mouth to his ear, making him look even more sinister. Jude saw that he had kind eyes and smiled back, wondering where someone who looked like a bouncer fitted into the set-up. Her first guess would have been that he was some sort of bodyguard, but Luca had called him 'friend' so that ruled that out.

'And this,' Luca began, urging the reluctant child forward, 'is Valentina, my daughter,' he explained, pride in his voice. 'Say hello to Signorina Lucas, Valentina.'

She did so in halting English, adding, 'I'm sorry my English is not so good.'

'It's a lot better than my Italian,' Jude said with a warm smile at the shy little girl. 'You have a very beautiful daughter, Mr Di Rossi.'

'Yes, I do.'

The little girl dimpled and blushed madly.

'Actually, Dr Lucas, it is fortuitous meeting you here. I was wanting to speak with you.'

'You did?' Whatever Luca wanted to say to her, Jude was sure she didn't want to hear it. 'I promised the children they could play on the swings,' she said quickly. 'Another time perhaps.'

As she turned away, calling the twins, strong fingers curled around her upper arm, cutting into her flesh through the cotton of her shirt.

'Now!'

Startled, she spun back. Her eyes collided with his and she could see the steely determination shining through his casual attitude.

'Valentina too is wanting to go to the playground. Carlo will take them whilst we have out little…chat.'

When he said it, 'chat' had a very sinister sound to it.

'You can have no fears about leaving the children in Carlo's care; he is more than capable. I would trust him with my Valentina's life.'

When Luca said something like that you got the impression he meant it quite literally.

'Well, after that recommendation what can I say?' she responded weakly. 'I'll keep Amy with me,' she told the big man when he approached her.

'Aunty Jude's going to get us a kite,' Jude heard Joseph boast to Valentina as they left under the watchful eye of the sinister-looking Carlo.

Despite Luca's reassurances Jude was still concerned. 'Does he work for you?'

'He worked for my father originally, but he has worked for me for some time.'

'Doing what?'

'He takes care of Valentina.'

'As a bodyguard?'

'That is part of his role, certainly. What is wrong now?' he asked, his impatient gaze fixed on her apprehensive face.

'Does he…is he…?' She lowered her voice to a confidential whisper. 'Does he carry a gun?'

'Several.'

Jude gave a gasp of alarm and then saw his expression. She coloured. 'You're joking.'

'I do not employ a private army who follow me around with bulging shoulder holsters—at least not in this country,' he delivered, straight-faced. 'Carlo,' Luca told her, 'is a gentleman in the true sense of the word. Now, shall we sit down?' he suggested, gesturing to a convenient park bench.

'I'd prefer to stand.'

Luca looked amused by her petty defiance. 'As you wish.'

'I didn't think my wishes came into it,' she remarked, rubbing her arm.

A frown formed on his formidably handsome features. 'I hurt you?'

'Don't worry, I'll survive.'

Their eyes locked. 'I am sorry,' he said stiffly. 'You are so tiny, delicate…' His glance flickered over her slender frame.

'But tough,' she promised him. Made uncomfortable by his intense scrutiny, she rushed into speech. 'Now, why don't you do us both a favour and say what you've got to? Though I really can't imagine what you want to talk to me about.'

He met her unfriendly and suspicious eyes. 'Are you always this prickly?'

'Prickly?'

'Touchy, irritable, belligerent…' he enumerated, ticking off these characteristics on the tanned fingers of his left hand.

'I am not—' she began, and then saw his expression. She bit her lip. 'I can just think of better things to do with my time.'

'Do I make you nervous?' he continued without giving her an opportunity to reply. 'You know what I think?'

Jude folded her arms across her chest. 'No, but I'm pretty

sure I'm about to find out,' she observed with a long-suffering sigh.

'I think you are antagonistic towards me because I witnessed your loss of control. You allowed me to see your vulnerability and now you are embarrassed about it,' he concluded with chilling detachment.

'Who gave you the right to stand there and dissect my feelings like I'm a specimen in a jar?' she demanded furiously.

'Afraid I'm muscling in on your professional territory?'

'Do you have a problem with psychologists?' she asked grimly. This was just the latest in a long line of sarcastic jibes on the subject.

'No, I have a problem with someone who needs help but is too stubborn to admit it.'

'And that's your professional opinion, is it?' At least he hadn't brought the wretched kiss into it.

His expressive shoulders lifted infinitesimally as he slanted an expectant glance towards her. 'And of course there is our unfinished business.'

Jude dealt him a look of loathing. 'There's nothing to finish because nothing started, and if you don't mind I've been trying not to think about what happened all night long so the last thing I want is some long drawn-out post-mortem now. It's not something I'm exactly proud of!'

'You're ashamed of your appetites?'

Put like that it made her sound an uptight bundle of repressions. 'I didn't say that!'

'If you're not proud, surely that means you are ashamed. But I digress…now, to what we are here for…'

'You mean it's not to insult me?'

'You have been left with the care of your brother's children. Your brother was a spender not a saver, and with share prices being as depressed as they are the value of what investments he did have has been more than halved.' His eyes sought Jude's for confirmation but she was too shocked to respond.

'The rest of the money is tied up in trusts for the children's education. There is the house, of course…' he mused. 'After the mortgage is paid off, how much would you say will be left over?'

With a sick feeling of dread in the pit of her stomach, she looked at him, her eyes wary. 'You tell me,' she replied hoarsely. 'You seem to be pretty well informed. *How*?' she added. 'How do you know all of this?' And why, she thought silently, did he want to?

'The how is not important.' He brushed aside her angry question impatiently.

'It is to me,' she promised. Though not as much as the much more perplexing 'why'…?

'You are in a situation from which there seems no deliverance.'

'I happen to have a well-paid job—not by your standards, maybe, but—'

'Ah, yes, your job,' he derided softly. 'The one you enjoy so much. You want to work.'

Her eyes narrowed. 'Is that a crime?'

'Not at all, but you no longer have just yourself to consider. You are faced with the dilemma of a working mother. High-cost child care, the needs of the children balanced against your desire for a career?'

All true and very depressing, though until he'd so eloquently summarised it she had managed to put it to the back of her mind. 'Listen, where exactly is this going?' she interrupted, seriously alarmed to hear him calmly discussing things she'd avoided thinking about herself so far.

'I have a suggestion to put to you, a solution…'

'Why would you want to help me?'

'Marry me.'

A strangled laugh emerged from Jude's throat. She tried to walk away—she didn't exactly relish being the target of some sort of sick joke—but she appeared to have lost most of her voluntary motor function.

'The idea of marriage to me is so amusing?' He didn't sound particularly put out.

'I take it that is what passes as a joke where you come from?' she finally managed hoarsely. 'I suppose the next thing you'll be telling me is you have fallen desperately in love with me?' She gave a slightly wild laugh.

'I would not insult you by suggesting anything so absurd.'

'*Thank you*,' she returned drily.

'I,' he announced, 'am your way out of a difficult situation.'

'My white knight, in fact…' she suggested.

He watched sombrely as she smiled as if at a private joke. 'If you like,' he conceded with the air of a man willing to humour her. 'If you marry me you will be free to pursue your career untroubled by concerns for the children. They will be well provided for.'

'You mean you're going to give up your job and become a house-husband? How very modern,' she trilled admiringly. He looked serious, he sounded serious, but logic told her he couldn't possibly be.

Her frivolity caused his brows to draw into a dark line of disapproval. 'I am getting the feeling that you're not taking this seriously.'

'And that surprises you?' Jude buried her face in her hands and then slid her hands downwards until just her eyes were revealed. 'Tell me, Luca, do I look mad?'

He seemed to consider her satirical question an invitation to search her face. 'No,' he pronounced after several uncomfortable moments of searching scrutiny. 'You look exhausted. Did the children not have a good night?'

'No, I…' She stopped; she could hardly explain that she'd spent the entire night reliving his kiss. It didn't matter how hard she'd tried to fill her head with other things, she hadn't been able to blank it out. 'Didn't sleep,' she ended abruptly.

'Neither did I,' he supplied surprisingly.

But not for the same reason as me, she thought despondently. It didn't seem fair that he was the picture of glowing health and vitality after his sleepless night whilst she, by his own mouth, looked terrible.

He bent and picked up a toy that Amy had thrown from the pushchair, giving Jude a view of the back of his head and neck. Her oversensitive stomach muscles clenched as she observed the way his dark hair curled into his nape. He straightened up and Jude quickly lowered her gaze.

From under her lashes she watched him smile and return the toy to the child. That smile held none of the sneering arrogance he reserved for her, and suddenly Jude was seized by an irrational desire for him to smile at her that way. Amy might not have understood a word of the Italian he spoke, but she was clearly charmed by it. Jude watched the interchange, marvelling at the alteration in the man when he was around children.

'Well, as you're not about to announce your undying love for me, perhaps we should get down to what this is really about.' She folded her arms across her chest and adopted what she hoped was a suitably hard boiled expression. 'What would you get from marrying me?'

'I get insurance.'

'Insurance?' she echoed blankly.

'My daughter's grandparents are trying to contest custody of Valentina, or, at least,' he corrected, 'their son and his wife are.'

'Why would they do that?' Jude asked, startled.

'Because they think I'm a bad father?'

'No!' Jude responded without thinking.

A look she couldn't quite analyse passed across his dark face. 'Thank you,' he said quietly.

Jude blushed. 'Well, you obviously love your daughter even if you are…'

'A womanising rat with a reputation for violence? That,' he continued smoothly before Jude could agree with or deny his analysis, 'is exactly my problem.'

'What about Valentina's mother? I assume you are not together?'

'We were *never* together.'

The peculiar emphasis in his voice made Jude frown. 'But surely she has some say.'

'She is dead.'

Jude's eyes softened with sympathy. 'Oh, I'm sorry. How? Sorry.' She shook her head with embarrassment. 'I didn't mean to pry.'

'I have just asked you to marry me, you are allowed to pry—a little.' This qualification made it clear there were limits to how far her curiosity would be tolerated. 'Maria killed herself just after Valentina was born. Apparently she was suffering from a severe form of post-natal depression.'

'Post-natal psychosis.'

He nodded. 'Unfortunately the condition went undiagnosed.'

Which would explain his antagonism towards her profession; many people lumped together psychiatry and psychology. 'That's terrible.'

'And in the past.'

Jude found herself wondering if he dismissed the past because it held too many painful memories. Had he loved Valentina's mother so much that it hurt to recall what he had lost?

'You know, I really don't think you have anything to worry about,' she reflected, so caught up in the story he had told that for a moment she forgot why he was telling her.

'That's all right, then.'

Her lips tightened at his derisive tone. 'Unless the stories of your financial empire have been exaggerated?' Her brows lifted as she shot him an interrogative glare to which he responded with an almost amused shake of his head. 'Well, in that case I'm sure you can afford the best legal advice there is.'

'I can, and it agrees with you—I would most likely win a court battle. However a court battle would be a messy business and dredge up a number of things I'd prefer stayed buried.'

'I'm not surprised, under the circumstances,' she admitted thoughtlessly. 'It must be awful to read things like that about yourself in the newspapers.'

She heard his stark inhalation and looked up to find his piercing gaze of displeasure fixed upon her face.

'It isn't *my* embarrassment I'm concerned about,' he told her, continuing to regard her as though she were something unpleasant on his shoe. 'I would like to save Valentina from being the focus of speculation and unwanted media attention.'

'I agree it is terribly unfair that innocent members of the family suffer for the failings of one person. Perhaps you should have thought of that before you—'

'My *failings*?' His incredulous echo cut through her critical condemnation. 'So my daughter is suffering because of my sins?' he enquired, his glittering gaze fixed on her face.

Jude didn't see why she should back down. 'Well, I'm sorry if you don't like it, but it seems to me that for someone who complains about it you do seem to court publicity.'

His eyes narrowed. 'You may well be right. But think about this,' he suggested in a silky, lethal voice. 'I take a stroll in the park, I sit down and chat to a pretty girl with—' he paused to murmur something soft in Italian to Amy '—a baby,' he added, his eyes hardening as they swivelled to Jude.

'The next day I wake up to discover I have a love-child and

you and your friends are being doorstepped by so-called journalists for details of your affair.'

Jude's eyes had widened to their fullest extent. 'You're not serious, they couldn't?' His dark brows lifted. 'Could they?' She couldn't help glancing over her shoulder. Then laughed nervously at her own foolishness. 'That would be dishonest.'

Her relieved comment caused Luca to throw back his head and laugh. 'Are you *really* that naïve?' he wondered, the amusement fading from his face.

'I'm not naïve,' she denied, stung by the accusation.

'Don't knock it, it's a rare quality.'

Jude, her thoughts still revolving around the life he had described, didn't register his response. The idea of a life where what you had for dinner was a story filled her with horror.

She shook her head. 'How do you live that way? I think I'd want to hide away behind tall walls patrolled by armed guards.'

'That is one solution, certainly,' he agreed.

'But not yours?'

His head moved fractionally in acknowledgement. 'I take security precautions.' He shrugged. 'I would be a fool not to, but the opinion of strangers has never been something which has kept me awake nights.' Again the inimical shrug. 'Life is too short.'

'Lucky you.'

He shot her a sharp look as if suspecting her of sarcasm, but he found only wistful envy in her face.

'You worry about what people think of you?'

'Everyone does…' she began, then with a wry smile corrected herself. 'Except you.'

'Do you worry what people will say when you marry me?'

She couldn't let him get away with that one. 'Don't you mean *if*?'

He bared his teeth in a wolfish smile and shook his head. 'No,' he replied simply.

What did a person do when faced with such impregnable self-belief? 'You just decide something's going to happen and assume that it will, don't you?'

'I have a positive attitude to life.'

Jude was torn between laughter and tears; the man was totally unbelievable. 'That's what I used to think about me, before I met you.' She hard the rising note of hysteria in her voice and took a deep, steadying breath before continuing. 'In answer to your question, people who know me know I have no intention of ever marrying. They would never believe it.'

'Well, if that concerns you, you will just have to convince them that falling desperately in love has altered your whole perception.'

The colour drained from Jude's face as she shook her head. 'That's ludicrous,' she responded faintly.

'It is,' he agreed. 'But I think you'll find that people generally accept *love* as being a perfectly valid excuse for aberrant behaviour that under normal circumstances would see you sectioned under the Mental Health Act,' he observed with a contemptuous sneer.

'Did I miss something here? Did I say yes to you and not notice?' She slanted a frustrated look at his bronzed chiselled face. 'Why me? Why marry me?'

'You have the children.'

This had gone beyond surreal. 'An instant family unit.'

Hearing the edge of hysteria creep in her shrill question, Luca shot a wary glance at her averted profile.

'Wouldn't it be more practical…?' Jude laughed and lifted a hand to her brow. What was she saying, *practical*…? Could there be a less appropriate term to use when describing such a totally insane proposition? She exhaled a gusty sigh and continued in a more composed tone. 'More…more rational,' she corrected, 'to marry someone you already know, someone you've…?'

A flicker of amusement crossed his dark features as her expressive face was suffused with colour. 'Slept with?'

Seeing him enjoying her embarrassment, Jude lifted her chin. 'Well, it would make a lot more sense.'

'The sort of qualities which make my lovers desirable companions are not those I am looking for in a wife.'

'I don't think I want to know what those are!' Jude exclaimed in an accent of outrage. Then almost immediately contradicted herself by demanding angrily, 'I suppose you think wives should be placid, undemanding creatures who don't mind their husbands seeking their excitement elsewhere!' she accused with disgust.

'You misunderstand me,' Luca replied, thinking he had rarely seen anything less placid than his proposed bride's impassioned face.

Jude snorted. 'My wife doesn't understand me—not very original! And we're not even married yet. Not,' she added hastily, 'that we're going to be.'

'We are,' he promised her. 'you just haven't admitted it yet.'

God, what did she have to do to get it through to him she wasn't going to say yes? Jude wondered helplessly. She suspected it would probably take a bomb to puncture his hermetically sealed confidence.

'When was the last time someone said no to you?'

A dangerous glint appeared in his dark eyes. 'Last night, as it happens.'

'Listen, I'm not going to marry you. There are no circumstances in this world that would make me say yes! *None!*' she yelled. 'I'm going to find the children and if you follow me I'll have you arrested for stalking,' she threatened him wildly.

CHAPTER SIX

JUDE picked up the phone for the fourth time in as many minutes, her face creased with indecision.

'This is stupid,' she told herself. 'I'm going to ring him.'

After all, what was the worst that could happen if she called out the doctor and it was a false alarm? He would think she was a time-wasting neurotic woman who couldn't distinguish a tummy bug from a life-threatening illness. If on the other hand it wasn't a tummy bug and she didn't seek medical help—well, when you thought about it that way there was no choice.

The doorbell rang just when the mechanical voice the other end was telling her that the surgery was closed and giving her an alternative number to ring if it was an emergency. Jude, who couldn't imagine why anyone would ring a doctor's surgery at this time of night if it weren't an emergency, repeated the number under her breath whilst she tried to find an elusive pen—the one she *always* kept by the phone.

The doorbell in the background kept on ringing. With an exclamation of irritation she ran across the room and flung it open, still repeating the numbers under her breath like a mantra.

'Go away,' she snapped at the tall figure, then added, catching hold of his arm, 'No, don't…'

'I wasn't going to,' Luca replied, his perceptive glance moving thoughtfully over her face.

'Have you got a pen?'

This terse demand made Luca blink. 'A pen?'

Jude ran her fingers through her hair in frustration. 'Yes, a pen, the thing you write with.' Closing her eyes to concentrate, she began repeating the number under her breath.

It was a few moments later, when she had the number written down, that she started to see how her behaviour might have seemed a little strange.

'Thank you,' she said, handing Luca his pen back.

'Keep it.'

Jude didn't lower her hand, their eyes touched, and though there was a flicker of irritation at the back of his eyes he shrugged and took it off her.

'I had thought you might enjoy a little adult company once the children had gone to bed,' he observed as he tucked the pen back into his inside pocket. His eyes lifted. 'But it looks as though I disturbed you,' he acknowledged, his eyes skimming the cotton nightdress she wore even though it was still only ten p.m.

'You always disturb me.' Jude didn't even register what she had said, let alone the effect her words had had upon Luca. 'Oh, my God, I don't believe this,' she groaned in frustration when she got an engaged signal. Receiver clutched to her chest, she ran a hand across her face and was surprised to discover the wetness of tears.

'What is the matter?'

She lifted her head. 'Are you still here?' She looked at the bottle of wine in his hand and gave a bitter smile. 'Sorry, it looks like I've ruined your seduction scene.'

Her attempts to redial were frustrated by a large hand that depressed all the keys.

'Tell me who you are ringing with such urgency.' His brows drew together in a straight line. 'A boyfriend?'

'A boyfriend?' she repeated as though he were mad. 'I'm ringing a doctor. At least,' she added wryly, 'I'm trying to.'

'A doctor! Are you ill?'

She shook her head. 'Not me, Joseph—at least, I think he is. It's probably nothing, but I—'

He closed the door and immediately his overpowering presence filled the tiny vestibule. 'Tell me.' When she showed reluctance he added, 'Sometimes it helps get things in perspective to have another person there as a sounding-board.'

Jude would have dearly loved to tell him to go to hell, but the fact was he was right and this was no time to be allowing personal animosity to dictate her actions.

Animosity…is that what you call it? She shook her head to silence the ironic laughter.

She sighed. 'All right, I suppose you'd better come through, but keep it down,' she added, nodding to the figure curled up under a duvet on the sofa. 'Sophia,' she explained. 'Joseph wanted to come in with me when he couldn't settle, but there wasn't much room so I popped Sophia on my bed.'

'You're sleeping on a sofa?' He sounded appalled.

'Only temporarily,' she gritted defensively. She perched on the arm of chair as far away from the sleeping child as possible and, eyes fixed on her bare feet, she began to recount the sequence of events over the past couple of hours.

'I went to bed after the children fell asleep about eight,' she explained. Ironically the idea had been to catch up on some lost sleep. 'Joseph woke me about half an hour later. He wanted to get into bed with me—they do sometimes. About half an hour later he started complaining of tummy pains and he was really hot. He seems to be drifting in and out of sleep now…I didn't know what to do, wait until morning or call out the doctor…'

Luca's response was immediate and straightforward. 'Well, if you have any doubts whatever obviously you must get a medical opinion.'

She gave a sigh, relieved to have her decision validated. 'What if the doctor won't come out?' she questioned, revealing another anxiety. 'It'll probably be hours before he gets here anyway. Perhaps I should take him straight to Casualty or one of those drop-in places?'

'Traipse a sick child across the city in the middle of the night?'

'You don't think it's a good idea, then? Has Valentina ever been sick in the middle of the night?'

'All children have been sick in the middle of the night—it is in their remit.' Luca looked at her pale, distressed face and then without a word withdrew a phone from his pocket. 'Another thing all children have in common is their recuperative powers,' he said before punching in a number.

The conversation was short and conducted in Italian. 'A doctor is coming.'

A wave of relief washed over her. 'Just like that?'

'He is a friend.' He stopped as Joseph's distressed cries rang out.

'I want my mummy!'

In that split second before she broke eye contact it had all been there in her eyes for Luca to see—the desperate pain and anguish. And then even before his brain had told him what he was seeing she was turning away, a hand pressed to her trembling lips.

Under the thin covering of cotton he could make out the shadowy curve of her spine and the feminine flare of her hips. He watched her hunched shoulders heave and was gripped by an overpowering desire to take away the problems that weighed her down. The strength of feeling astonished him.

For the first time he saw her as more than a means of solving his problem or a woman whom he had found himself strongly—*extremely* strongly—attracted to. He saw someone who was facing a bad time in her life with guts.

'It does get better, you know.'

His soft words made her lift her head. 'Oh, God, don't say anything nice to me,' she begged him, 'or I'll cry. I have to go to Joseph, he needs me…' She smiled awkwardly. 'And thank you for organising the doctor; it was—kind of you.' The perplexed frown that pleated her brow spoke volumes.

'Is there anything else I can do?'

'You can leave that if you like,' she said, nodding to the bottle in his hand.

Luca's own eyes drifted in the same direction; slowly he began to shake his head. 'Drinking alone is not a good habit to get into.' For a second she thought he was adding secret drinker to the list of faults he must have ticked off beside her name. Then he placed the bottle on the table and said. 'It stays, I stay.'

Jude, already halfway across the room, stopped and turned. 'That's really not—' Joseph cried out again and she bit her lip, threw one last confused look over her shoulder and hurried away.

By the time she had settled Joseph she could hear the soft, subdued sound of deep male voices in the other room.

'The doctor has come to see you, Joseph.'

'I don't want to see a doctor,' the child replied crankily just as two figures, preceded by a soft knock, entered the room. 'I don't like you,' he proceeded to tell the first figure, who Jude was astonished to see was magnificently attired in full black-tie glory. The significance of this outfit filled Jude with embarrassed dismay. Had Luca wielded the big stick and dragged the poor man away from a special occasion?

'Well, my first impressions of you are not all that favourable either,' she was amused to hear the man with slate-grey hair and dark eyes respond as he sat down on the edge of the bed. If he resented being dragged here he was hiding it well, she decided in relief.

'Though my friend, Luca here, tells me you are his friend also,' he added, casting a professional eye over the child's flushed face. 'So maybe we should try to get on.'

Jude saw the little boy flash a quick look at the second man; he received an almost imperceptible nod in return. 'All right, then. Where is Luca going?' he added, a note of panic in his shrill voice. 'I want Luca to stay.'

'I am going to make your aunt a cup of tea whilst the doctor here examines you. You must be a special patient because Dr Greco doesn't normally come to see people at home. I will see you a little later,' he promised as he made his exit.

Jude was impressed at how well the doctor handled the fretful little boy, and his eventual assessment, after a thorough but gentle examination, that there was nothing serious wrong beyond a mild stomach bug brought a relieved smile to her lips. She felt as though the weight of a small continent had been lifted from her shoulders.

'I could kiss you,' she admitted with a happy sigh as they left the room.

'I don't think Luca would like that,' the medic commented with an amused twinkle in his eyes.

'I wouldn't like what?'

Jude jumped and her heart started to thump a little faster.

'Me, kissing your bride to be.'

'Jude hasn't said yes yet, Alex,' Luca spelt out, a thread of annoyance in his deep voice. 'But you're right, I wouldn't like it, and neither I suspect would Sonia? Talking of whom, if you hurry you'll just make the second act.'

The other man rumbled something in Italian and turned back to Jude, who hadn't moved a muscle since she'd heard herself referred to as Luca's bride to be. Just how many people had he shared this misinformation with?

'Just keep him on clear fluids,' she heard the doctor advise when she tuned back into the conversation.

She gave a tight little nod.

'And he'll bounce back in no time,' he added soothingly, quite obviously attributing her rigidity to lingering concerns. 'But if you've got any worries,' he continued, 'don't hesitate to call me. Luca has my number.' He nodded and banged the taller man on the back.

'I feel terrible about bothering you over nothing,' Jude admitted huskily. 'And I've obviously ruined your evening,' she said her pained gaze fixed upon his elegant outfit.

It was amazing how well Italian men wore clothes, she reflected, sliding a secret sideways glance towards the other Italian in the room. Now he would look simply magnificent similarly clad, not that he looked half bad as he was, she admitted, repressing an appreciative sigh.

'Actually you saved me from a interminable evening,' he told her frankly. 'My wife,' he explained in response to her sceptical expression, 'is the opera buff. I—according to her—am the philistine. I usually disgrace myself by falling asleep. Now is there somewhere I could wash my hands?'

Jude directed him to the bathroom. That left her alone with Luca; the sleeping child's presence could be safely discounted. And being alone with Luca scared her witless.

Did one piece of kindness cancel out the acres of unacceptable behaviour that went before? Her most immediate problem seemed to be what did she do first: thank Luca or strongly protest him going around telling the world she was going to marry him? There was a limit to the time you could pretend someone wasn't there and she had already exceeded it.

She took a deep breath, exhaled and turned her head.

It didn't take her long—long as in about five seconds of contact with those almost unbelievably seductive eyes—to figure out that she'd been totally wrong about her immediate problem. That status went to the charged atmosphere that was building up between them.

The build-up of tension in the air between them was almost palpable; the air, thick with it, crackled.

'I'm glad it's nothing serious. You were thinking appendicitis?'

'It crossed my mind. I suppose you think that's stupid of me?' We're talking, she thought, and everything sounds normal, but it's window dressing—just below the surface the tensions still seethe.

'Valentina had a headache and a gnat bite on her leg. I rushed her to a casualty department with suspected meningitis.'

A giggle was drawn from her. 'You didn't!'

One corner of his mouth lifted a sardonic half-smile. 'No,' he admitted, 'I didn't, but only because there was a consultant paediatrician staying to dinner.'

Her eyes widened. 'Dr Greco?'

He nodded. 'He is Valentina's godfather.'

'What did he say to you back there, when he spoke Italian?' she suddenly blurted out.

A veil came down over his expressive eyes. 'I'm sorry—we didn't mean to exclude you.'

'What did he say, Luca?'

'He said having to do the running for once might teach me a bit of humility. He seemed to like the idea of me running after a woman who wasn't interested. Only you are interested, aren't you, Jude?'

A surge of weakness washed over her. The sudden desire to concede defeat and have the weight of responsibility lifted off her shoulders was enormous.

She was perfectly well aware that any number of women would equate what she was being offered with winning the jackpot on the lottery. She would be universally envied her wealthy, incredibly handsome husband. There was only one element in the happy-ever-after equation missing…

'I think, all things considered, you should look elsewhere for your insurance policy.'

A spasm of irritation crossed his face. 'I want a wife, not an insurance policy.'

'You want a wife who is an insurance policy,' she countered wearily.

'Semantics apart, what are these "things" you have considered?'

Something inside Jude snapped; she was just too tired to take part in this clever play on words any longer. 'You really want to know? Fine, I'll tell you. I'm interested in you, not marriage, and you're interested in marriage, not me. I'd say those differences are pretty irreconcilable.'

Ironically if she'd hadn't fallen in love with him it might have worked. In theory, acknowledging her feelings should have been an empowering experience; in reality she had rarely felt less in control of her fate in her life. It was easy to see why repressing was so popular!

'But whilst you're looking for someone more suitable, if you like we could…not when you find someone else, of course,' she added hastily. 'But until then…?'

'While I am looking?' An expression of total astonishment washed across his face. 'You are saying…?' He raked a hand through his sleek dark hair and gave a strange laugh before restarting in a slow, carefully measured tone. 'You are saying that you want to be my mistress but not my wife?'

'I wouldn't have put it exactly like that, but I suppose that about sums it up,' she admitted.

'*Dio!*' he ejaculated rawly as his glittering dark eyes raked her face. 'You never fail to surprise me, *cara*. You have given this matter some thought, it seems?'

Jude caught her full lower lip between her teeth and turned her attention to her bare feet. 'I haven't thought about much else but you since we met.' Had someone put a truth drug in her cocoa this evening?

The sound of his harsh inhalation brought her attention back to his face. 'You are tired and stressed.' His voice sounded oddly stilted.

'Oh, God, I've embarrassed you!' She gave a mortified groan. 'I'm so sorry, take no notice of what I say,' she begged. 'You're right, erratic mood swings, irrational behaviour—it's all classic signs of sleep deprivation.'

Her babble was cut off by a finger laid against her lips. 'I am not embarrassed, *cara*. I am…' He suddenly took her face between his hands. 'I am in a state of almost constant arousal since I met you. When you make an offer like that I do not feel embarrassment, I feel pain,' he revealed with an earthy laugh, which deepened as her eyes slid downwards over his lean male body.

A wave of scalding heat had engulfed her from head to toe by the time her wandering gaze settled back on his face.

'You see I wasn't exaggerating.' His face was wiped clean of mocking humour when he leaned towards her. The feathery touch of his warm breath lightly brushed her cheek; it sent tiny electric shocks skimming across her skin. When he added in a throbbing, throaty whisper, 'I want to make love to you right here, right now.' Her body swayed towards him as though their bodies were attached by some invisible thread. 'What wouldn't I give for a few hours alone with you to show you just how strong that need is?'

It was difficult to speak when you were burning up with

lust and longing, but Jude forced the words out. Even the most desirable of situations—namely being lusted after by a man who turned you on just by breathing—had a downside.

'So you agree with my terms?' It wasn't necessary to speak above a whisper—the sides of their noses were almost grazing…their laboured breaths were intimately mingling.

'Hell, no!'

Jude's head jerked back. 'But you said—' she began to protest in agitation.

Luca slid a finger over the soft, full outline of her lips, effectively reducing her reasoning powers to nil. 'I said I want to make love to you. The only conditions that I abide by are my own.'

Jude had been crossing to the other side of the street to avoid men who liked to take charge and have it their own way all her life, and now she had fallen for a man whose arrogance was off the scale. Now *that* was irony!

'But you said…' she protested weakly.

'You think that I will take no for an answer now that I know you want me?'

'I thought you already knew that.'

He acknowledged her wry jibe with a tilt of his head. 'It's pleasing to hear you say it, *cara*. You will enjoy being my wife,' he promised. 'But,' he added, drawing himself upright, 'that is the last you will hear me say on the subject for the moment. You are tired, and nursing a sick child—it is not an atmosphere that lends itself to romance.'

So far it was lending itself pretty well. 'I can think of nothing less romantic than a marriage of convenience.'

His shoulders lifted in one of his elegant, peerless shrugs. 'A marriage of any sort is what two people make of it,' he claimed imperiously. 'Now to more immediate matters.' He picked up with a flourish a blanket that was draped over a threadbare overstuffed chair. 'I suggest you curl up in this chair and have a nap. I will wake you if Joseph needs you.'

'That's ludicrous.'

'Alex, Jude thinks it is ludicrous that she catches up on some sleep whilst I hold the fort. What is your professional opinion?'

Jude, who hadn't been aware of the doctor's entrance, gave him a quick smile and hoped he hadn't been standing there too long.

'My professional opinion is that you should take the opportunity to rest. My personal opinion,' he added, flashing a sly grin in the direction of the younger man, 'is that arguing with Luca is *always* a pointless and exhausting exercise. If argument fails he wears you down by attrition. Oh, and if you're worried about his welfare, don't,' he advised. 'Luca is one of those unnatural individuals who function perfectly well on a couple of hours' sleep.'

'Is this a conspiracy?' she asked, looking from one man to the other, her glance resting significantly longest on Luca. She was just too tired to resist or even think straight.

'Well, I'll go and check on Joseph and *maybe* I will take a short nap…' She stifled a yawn and pretended not to notice when the two men exchanged knowing glances. 'You promise you'll wake me if I'm needed.'

'You have my word.'

Jude awoke to the smell of coffee. She stretched, finding a number of painful knots in her spine.

'She's awake, she's awake!' a shrill voice carolled. 'Can I watch the cartoons now?'

Jude watched Sophia, a piece of toast in her hand, dance around the room in her favourite bunny pyjamas whilst she waited for a response to her bellow.

Jude had just pushed aside the blanket when Luca appeared.

The sight of his tall, vital figure jerked her from drowsiness to a full state of over-stimulated alert in two seconds flat!

Luca's jet eyes slid to hers and her oversensitive stomach went into a spiralling dive—my, God, but it wasn't fair that anyone could look that good on no sleep.

'Well, if she wasn't awake she is now. Do you mind?' he asked Jude. 'I did promise her.'

She gave a jerked abstracted, affirmative nod. 'You stayed all night,' she accused huskily.

Luca strolled over to the TV and turned it on with a firm, 'Half an hour only,' to the impatient child. 'I would have woken you, but Joseph settled well soon after you fell asleep. He woke up about half an hour ago asking for breakfast. He settled for juice and he's dozing again.'

'So you made a unilateral decision on my behalf.'

'It was hard to make any other sort when you were asleep.' He responded with maddening calm to her aggressive accusation. 'I can live with the snoring,' he added in a solemn aside.

'I do not snore, and it's not your job to look after my family.'

'I would like to make it my job.'

Jude couldn't think of a retort, cutting or otherwise, to this simple statement.

He gestured towards a laptop open on the table. 'I had some work to get through. I had it brought down, so you see I wouldn't have slept anyhow. It seemed more sensible for you to get some rest. I have not had time to bathe the baby…is something wrong?' he queried in response to the choking sound that emerged from her throat.

'The picture of The World's Most Notorious Playboy bathing a baby is kind of…surreal.'

He accepted her comment with a shrug. 'I had begun to think that maybe you were looking at me, not my public persona…'

'I am!' she protested unthinkingly as she stumbled sleepy-eyed to her feet. 'I think they give you a very hard time. If it was left to me I'd make sure those…' Belatedly becoming aware of his interested expression, she moderated her spirited defence and added awkwardly, 'It's just my father never had much to do with us…hands-on stuff, you know. You…Italian men seem more relaxed around children.'

My God, he stayed the night. I've spent the night with a gorgeous man and I'm still a virgin—this could only happen to me!

'Your father is alive? You should not keep coffee beans in the fridge,' he explained, planting a steaming mug on the occasional table beside her. 'It destroys the flavour.'

'Thank you,' she said quietly as she tried to smooth down her hair. 'My father lives overseas; my parents divorced when David and I were quite small. He has remarried, I have a half-brother and sister but I've never met them. We write…I write.' She gave a quick strained smile. 'He's not much of a writer.'

'When was the last time you saw him?'

'About five years ago. We speak on the telephone occasionally.' She gave a small brisk shrug and smiled to show that she was all right with the situation. 'Nice coffee,' she added, nursing the hot mug between her hands.

'Did he not come for your brother's funeral?'

'He wanted to, but apparently his wife was rushed into hospital just as he was about to board the plane. You were actually bang on when you said I was completely clueless about the hands-on stuff of parenting. I know all the theory, of course. I think being a decent parent is something you're born with.'

'I disagree. I think most people learn by a mixture of example and trial and error.'

'Well, I *definitely* didn't learn by example.'

'How so?'

She considered telling him to mind his own business and then thought—why not answer him? He was easy to talk to—

maybe, she mused, it was because he gave the impression that he was actually listening, a rare quality in her experience. Most men she knew were much happier talking about themselves.

'My mother is a partner in a successful—*very* successful— PR firm. We, David and me, didn't exactly see a lot of her either. I used to resent the fact she never had any time for us, but later on I appreciated that her working was what paid for the lifestyle I enjoyed. I expect,' she added, looking at him over the rim of her mug, 'it seems a bit strange to you, that sort of dysfunctional family. I suppose you've got an enormous extended family and hundreds of brothers and sisters, aunts and uncles…?'

A wistful note entered her voice as she envisaged an idealised big, noisy family where everyone laughed, loved and argued loudly but presented a united front to the world.

'There is just Marco and myself; he is my half-brother. My own mother died when I was very young, and my father never stopped loving her. This was not a situation which made my stepmother feel secure or inclined her to be particularly fond of me. Once Marco was born she did everything she could to isolate me. She saw me as a rival for my father's affections, which was foolish because he never actually noticed I was there.'

Behind this prosaic declaration Jude saw the years of hurt beyond the protective wall he had built up. 'Oh, Luca.'

The soft sound of her voice brought Luca's attention back to her face. 'I'm sorry to spoil your image of a warm, loving family.'

Her tender heart ached for the unloved boy he had been. 'Well, you have your own family now.'

'Yes, *we* have?'

'Luca!'

He took her chin between his thumb and forefinger and smiled down into her flustered face. 'I have an early meeting I cannot miss, and breakfast to take with Valentina.' He placed a hand on his flat midriff. 'You must come live with me—my waistline will not survive two breakfasts on a regular basis. Think about the practicalities and we will speak later.'

Jude sat there disconsolately after he had left. Did he think saving money on fuel bills was going to swing her undecided vote? A hissing sound of frustration escaped through her clenched teeth. She didn't want to think about practicalities; she wanted to think about love!

'Stupid man!'

'Who's stupid, Aunty Jude?' Sophia asked, climbing up onto her lap.

Me for falling in love with someone who thinks marriage is a merger, she thought. 'Nobody, darling,' she replied, stroking the little girl's soft curls.

CHAPTER SEVEN

AFTER she had finally shut the door on the two women Jude allowed her fixed smile to fade. She was literally shaking with fury. The aftermath of shock made her feel as if she was going to be physically sick. She closed her eyes, leaned her back against the wall and waited for the waves of nausea to pass.

When he'd said he wouldn't take no for an answer it had not occurred to Jude that Luca would resort to this sort of scummy underhand tactics. Which makes me, she thought furiously, exactly what he accused me of being—ridiculously naïve. She ought to have realised what he was capable of— you only had to look at him to see that he was totally ruthless and without scruples.

It just went to show children and animals were not the benchmark of approval people claimed. Children loved him and he was a traitorous rat! Well, no more, the gloves were off and she was going to fight fire with fire. If he thought that he could scare and intimidate her…

A troubled expression settled over her pale features as she pressed her fingers to her drumming temples. A fine sweat broke out all over her body as she recalled the heart-stopping shock and apprehension she had felt when the two women had introduced themselves as representatives of social services.

A 'concerned neighbour'—they couldn't say who, of course—it transpired, had reported children's distressed crying all through the night. *Concerned neighbour*. Rage rushed through Jude as she looked back at that terrible half-hour. It hadn't taken the ladies from social services long to satisfy themselves that the children were fit and healthy.

They were actually extremely sympathetic about the situation, but did express concern about the cramped conditions, which Jude hastened to assure them were only a stopgap. Despite their assurances that they were more than happy with how she was coping, the spectre of being considered an unfit parent had raised itself in Jude's head. She was going to spend the next ten years looking over her shoulder, waiting for someone with an official-looking document to arrive and whisk the children away—because quite frankly you're not up to the job, she told herself.

A sudden knock on the door jolted her from her reverie. Her eyes narrowed as she drew herself to her full height—all five feet two inches of it—and shook back her hair. No doubt he just couldn't resist coming to gloat…she would give him gloat!

She wrenched back the door, her bosom heaving, her eyes blazing, and stopped, a taken-aback expression stealing over her face. '*Mother!* What are *you* doing here?'

Lyn Lucas, who had looked equally taken aback to be greeted by a blazing figure of retribution, recovered her composure as she stepped into the flat. 'Well, really, Jude, is that any way to greet your mother?' Delicately she kissed the air either side of her daughter's face. 'Especially as I've cancelled several meetings to be here.' Her brow wrinkled delicately, as though she was faintly mystified by her own actions. 'What,' she added in horror, 'have you done with your hair?'

Jude lifted a vague hand to her curly head. 'Oh, nothing, literally,' she replied absently. 'Listen, Mum, you couldn't just hold the fort for a few minutes, could you? Thank you, that's great, marvellous…they can watch a cartoon video. Not the one in the machine—it scares Amy,' she yelled over her shoulder.

A look of total astonishment on her exquisitely made-up face, Lyn Lucas watched her daughter run off towards the lift.

'Granny Lyn!' a piercing young voice suddenly yelled. Squaring her narrow shoulders, Lyn Lucas stepped with fastidious care over the toys scattered across the wooden floor. 'Come and see what presents…Granny has for you, children,' she said, turning to her grandchildren with an attitude reminiscent of an early martyr.

Carlo opened the door. He took one look at Jude's stormy face and stepped aside to let her enter without asking for an explanation as to why she had presented herself unannounced.

'I will see if—' he began.

'Oh, he'll see me, all right!' Jude hissed, rounding like a spitting cat on the unfortunate retainer. She looked around the long hallway, her expression frustrated; there were at least a dozen doors leading off it. 'Where is he?'

'I believe he is in his bedroom, miss. Sixth door on the left, but—'

'Fine,' Jude flashed, baring her teeth in a savage grin as she turned on her heel and began counting off the doors under her breath as she passed them. 'One…*inevitable* I'll marry him! Two…the only *inevitable* thing is me strangling him with my own bare hands! Three, he's a manipulative, conniving rat!' By the time she had identified the correct door she had torn Luca's character to shreds and come to the conclusion that death was too good for him!

She took a deep breath and opened it without pause, not giving herself time to have second thoughts.

Luca lifted his head as the door banged against the wall behind it, causing the lamps set either side of the king-sized bed to shudder. The incredulous frown that drew his dark brows in a straight line relaxed into a quizzical expression as an avenging goddess—of diminutive stature—hands set on curvy hips, strode aggressively into his bedroom.

He lowered the towel he had been about to dry his hair with and looped it around his neck. 'To what do I owe this pleasure?' He suddenly stopped what he was doing. 'Is it Joseph?'

'No, he's fine…I…I…' If Jude had considered the possibility, which she hadn't, she might have recognised that if you walked into a man's bedroom unannounced there was a very definite possibility you might see more than you wanted.

If you don't like it, don't look, the sarcastic voice in her head suggested. Jude carried on staring.

What was not to like? He was quite simply…*sublime*! The muscles in her calves and thighs began to twitch and quiver the way they did after a long run; her breathing went the same way.

Thirty seconds might seem a long time when you were waiting for your nail varnish to dry, but when your eyes were welded on the gleaming bronzed body of a half-naked man it seemed way longer. Especially when it was the same man you only had to think about to become a mindless mass of craving hormones. *Way longer!*

'Like you don't know why I'm here!' she sneered, finally recovering the power of speech. Cheeks burning, she turned her back on him—*about thirty seconds too late*! Thirty seconds during which her complexion had gone through several dramatic colour changes and she had struggled to remember what she was here for.

She stood there drawing air into her oxygen deprived lungs in great gulping gasps. Closing her eyes, she just prayed that the faint rustles she could hear indicated he was putting on some clothes. If he had it wouldn't be because he felt awkward at being caught semi-naked—unlike her, Luca had been totally unselfconscious.

Obviously he had stepped out of the shower literally seconds before she'd walked in. He'd still been wet—a glazed expression slid into her half-closed eyes and a voluptuous little shudder slid down her spine as she recalled the drops of moisture from his drenched hair streaming down his face. Besides the towel around his neck and the other tiny one wound loosely about his narrow hips, he hadn't been wearing a stitch.

Water droplets clung to each smooth inch and every hard angle of his taut, toned body emphasising the already clear definition of his perfectly developed muscles. There was not an ounce of surplus flesh on his greyhound-lean frame. Her greedy gaze had eaten up the details. He possessed incredibly long legs roughened over the thighs by a dusting of dark body hair. There was a similar but denser sprinkling across his broad chest that narrowed down to an arrow strip across his washboard-flat belly.

She couldn't even think about the way he looked without experiencing another sharp stab of immobilising lust.

Of course Jude had been aware that he was a impressively built man, that much was evident in the grace and controlled power of his slightest movement or gesture. Actually seeing with her own eyes *just how* impressive and powerful was something that it would take a very unusual woman not to be affected by, she told herself.

Despite Jude's stubborn efforts, it was hard to rationalise and impersonalise the effect Luca had upon her—there was something *extremely* personal about the knot of heat low in her belly.

'Tales of my omnipotence have been greatly exaggerated, so perhaps you'd like to fill me in… How is Joseph this afternoon?'

Even before he came into view the hairs on the back of her

neck had informed her of his silent approach. As he walked past her Jude caught the clean male scent of him and experienced the pleasure-pain feeling again.

'Pretty rich to complain when it's the people you pay to promote you who most probably started the rumours of your omnipotence.'

He came to a halt a few feet in front of her wearing, to her immense relief, a robe in a silky black fabric.

A flicker of distaste passed over his lean features. 'I am not a commodity to be promoted.'

'Did I offend you? So sorry.' Her voice dripped malicious insincerity.

His eyes narrowed as he scanned her angry face. One dark brow lifted in sardonic enquiry. 'What is it I am meant to know, Judith?'

'Don't call me that,' she snapped. 'My name is Jude.'

He gave a very Latin shrug. 'I like Jude too.'

'*You* can call me Dr Lucas, and don't play the innocent with me.' Anything *less* innocent than the raw, earthy image of male virility he presented right now would be hard to imagine. 'You don't have a scruple in your entire body, do you? You'll do whatever it takes to get what you want and to hell with anyone else who gets hurt in the process…'

As he listened to her unflattering description of his character Luca's sardonic gaze continued to drift down to her passionately heaving bosom. He looks and I react, she thought, helpless to control the response of her own flesh to the brush of his lustrously lashed eyes.

'Finished?' he asked when she paused for breath.

'I've not even got warmed up yet,' she promised him grimly.

'Well, if this is going to be a long job why don't you make yourself more comfortable?' He inclined his head towards a sofa that was set against one wall. 'Or,' he added, a gleam appearing in his brooding, deep-set eyes, 'would you be more comfortable here?' he wondered, patting the opulent-looking bed.

Jude's eyes followed his gesture and a sharp thrill of excitement zapped through her body. The image that flashed through her head of tumbled bedclothes, and tangled limbs gleaming with sweat, made her throat close over. It was several moments before she trusted herself to respond.

'I think that you're comfortable enough for us both,' she choked, unable to control the movement of her eyes as they hungrily travelled down his long, lean, muscle-packed length.

'I'd have dressed,' he promised drily, 'if I'd known I was having a guest.'

She knew it was impossible, but when he looked at her *that* way... God, maybe he actually could read her mind! Even thinking the impossible made her stomach tie itself into terrified knots. *What's wrong with me? The man's not a mind-reader, he's just a monster.*

'Don't worry, I won't be staying long—I just came to tell you it didn't work.' She schooled her expression into something approaching boredom. 'The social workers could see that the children are well cared for—' she sniffed, her voice thickening emotionally '—*and loved...*'

He shook his head slightly with a look of blank incomprehension. *He's very good,* she marvelled bitterly. *If I didn't know he was lying through his teeth I'd believe him myself.*

'Social workers?'

An explosive sound of frustration escaped from between her tightly pursed lips. 'Yes, the ones *you* reported me to. You have to be the lowest form of life ever to crawl out of the primeval slime and draw breath, and if you think you can frighten me...blackmail me into marrying you... Well, think again,' she declared defiantly. 'After your act last night and this morning I actually started thinking I hadn't been fair to you. I thought you were pretty heroic being so supportive and not taking advantage of me when you had the opportunity because I was vulnerable. That was a stroke of pure genius. I was *touched* by your restraint—how funny is that?'

'If it makes you feel any happier I spent most of the night regretting my…erm…*restraint*,' he interjected. 'I am a little confused—last night you revealed a desire to be my mistress?'

She saw his eyes were glittering and realised that underneath the sardonic mask he was not nearly so laid-back about this as he was pretending. Maybe he hadn't reckoned on her finding out. The irony was he hadn't needed the extra insurance; she'd been ready to say yes.

'Something,' she told him in a shaking voice, 'that I can't think about without being physically sick with shame! Are you listening to me?' she demanded as she wrathfully identified an expression in his face that suggested he had tuned her out. She raised her voice. 'Am I keeping you awake? I'm terribly sorry if I'm boring you.' Her lethal sarcasm appeared unappreciated.

'You have had a visit from social…what are these people called?' he demanded with a click of his fingers that suggested he was impatient that his extensive vocabulary had let him down on this occasion.

'Services,' she snapped, tapping her toe on the floor.

'Services…' With an air of purpose that created a draft he walked straight past her to the door, which he opened. She noticed he left damp footprints on the waxed wooden surface.

Her eyes tracked upwards from his feet and hair-roughened calves over the areas barely concealed by the sexy black robe. Her stomach muscles cramped as imagining what the black silk concealed sent a flash of heat over her skin.

How, she wondered despairingly, was it possible to loathe someone and ache for them in every fibre of your body at the same time?

Watching him with an air of studied disinterest, she was struck once more by the incredible energy the man projected. He was like a force of nature—unstoppable—like a hurricane. Like the hurricane, when he ripped your life apart you couldn't help being fascinated by the sheer beauty of the elemental force that had inflicted the destruction.

Standing with one foot in the hallway and one in the room, he yelled something in Italian. Carlo's deep voice replied in the same language. He turned back to Jude.

She held up her hand. 'Don't waste your time or breath,' she advised cynically. 'I'm well aware that Carlo would swear on a stack of bibles he was the Prince of Wales if you asked him to. Though what the hell you've done to inspire such devotion in a decent man beats me.'

'Carlo is a deeply religious man. He would not lie with his hand on the bible. He likes you too, which is unusual,' he admitted with a thoughtful expression. 'Normally he does not care for my female friends.'

To be lumped together with his trophy girlfriends was just too much for Jude, who went a pretty shade of pink. 'I am *not* your friend!' she announced in a revolted tone. 'And,' she added, 'I am not a girl...that is, I am a girl, just not in this context.'

Luca stood there listening with an expression of polite interest and showed no inclination to help her out as her garbled explanation became more fragmented.

'Oh, you know what I mean,' she finally concluded, wringing her hands in exasperation.

'Only for about fifty per cent of the time,' he admitted. Then added before she could respond, 'Mrs Montgomery.'

Jude gave an irritated shake of her head. 'I don't know any Mrs Montgomery.'

'I believe she lives in the apartment above you...?'

'She might do.' Jude shrugged. 'I've lived here twelve months and Marco is the only person I've had a conversation with and he only talked to me because he…' She stopped and blushed.

'You don't need to explain. You are female and have a pulse, that would qualify you.'

Jude's chin went up. 'I was going to say he found me attractive.'

'I suppose,' he conceded, 'that is not impossible.'

Jude folded her arms across her chest and issued an embittered, thin-lipped smile. 'You're *too* kind.'

'Did Marco invite you in here?' Despite his throw-away tone, the look he slanted her was strangely intent.

'This bedroom, you mean?'

His dark eyes flashed and Jude realised that she had unwittingly angered him, which was ironic because when she'd been trying she hadn't managed to. 'You are well aware of what I am asking—do not be obtuse.'

Jude could have quite legitimately claimed innocence because she didn't have a clue what he was getting at, but instead she shrugged and said, 'I'll be whatever I like.' And if you don't like it, all the better, she thought, in keeping with the childish theme as her unwillingly curious gaze swept around the large room for the first time.

Sunlight streamed in through three sets of patio doors that led out onto a large roof terrace giving the room, despite the dark wood underfoot, an extremely pleasant, light, airy feel. Other than the bold original artwork on the walls, the rugs scattered over the gleaming floor were the only splashes of colour in an otherwise subdued-hued room. Equal restraint was evident in the furnishings of what was a sparingly, but expensively equipped room.

The splendid king sized *lit bateau* with its intricately carved frame was the one feature that didn't follow the 'less is more' rule. The decadent piece dominated the room, or it would have if the owner had not been present.

'You like?'

She looked up to discover his eyes on her face.

She shrugged but was unable to prevent her eyes straying back to the suggestive bed. A guilty flush mounted her cheeks.

'It says more about the bank balance than the man,' she offered nastily, 'but then that's always supposing there actually is any substance in the man—that he isn't just a pretty face and a set of well-developed pecs…?'

There was a moment's startled silence before Jude was frustrated to find her insults had fallen on unappreciative ears—nobody witnessing his burst of spontaneous laughter would have assumed he was cut to the quick!

Looking at him with his head thrown back to reveal the strong brown lines of his throat, it occurred to her that if any photographer had been in a position to capture that image it would have made his career. The human and *extremely* attractive image of a man famed for his iron control.

She might not possess the picture but Jude, experiencing a sudden flash of insight, knew that the image was indelibly imprinted into her brain. How many times at some future date will I remember this moment and think—I could have married him?

Would she regret the decision…?

What would David say if he knew that the incredibly famous and wealthy playboy had proposed to the little sister he'd called Judy? Would he have congratulated her on standing by her principles? Not likely, not David! He would have spotted her true feelings before she had.

You've had a better offer, have you, Judy? She could almost hear her brother's dry voice.

'Then this isn't a style you are comfortable with?' Luca's

deeper voice, still tinged by the amusement, interrupted her moment of soul-searching.

'I find the minimalist look in a bedroom a little cold myself,' lied Jude, who knew that any room that held Luca and *that* bed was never going to feel cold to her!

Luca ran a hand through his dark hair, a hint of impatience creeping into his expression. 'I asked you a question,' he reminded her.

'I've forgotten what it was.'

'I asked has Marco ever invited you in here.'

'Why would Marco invite me into your bedroom?'

A hissing sound escaped through his clenched teeth. *'Have you slept with my brother?'* he rapped in a voice like a steel trap.

Jude's mouth fell open as slowly heat began to seep into her pale face until it was burning. 'I'd say that's none of your damned business.'

'On the contrary, as the man you're going to marry I'd say it is quite definitely my business,' he contradicted smoothly. 'You know,' he mused, 'for a psychologist you have a very uptight attitude to sex.'

Just when Jude had been about to rebut this outrageous claim—both of them!—he added in a honey-coated drawl that sent secret little shivers up and down her spine, 'There should be no secrets between us, *cara*.'

'Does that mean you're going to give me chapter and verse on all your mistresses?' She gave a caustic laugh and felt sick as her fevered imagination supplied images of Luca in that bed with one of the innumerable beauties she'd seen hanging on his arm in news articles. 'I really don't have the stomach, or for that matter the odd month to spare, for that!'

Dark eyes scanned her flushed face and abruptly the frown lifted. 'You are jealous,' he discovered.

CHAPTER EIGHT

BEFORE Jude could smack Luca's smug face, or hotly disclaim this preposterous claim—or both—he seamlessly picked up the theme he had dropped earlier. It made Jude dizzy just trying to keep pace with his thought processes.

'I mention Mrs Montgomery,' he explained, nothing in his manner suggesting he'd been interrogating her about her sex life seconds earlier, 'because apparently we had a visit from that lady earlier this week, or so Carlo tells me. I was not at home.'

Jude, who found the name conjured an image of a rather stern, hatchet-faced woman, thought he might have been lucky.

'I understand most of the other residents were treated to a visitation too.'

'Well, I wasn't, and I really don't see what this has got to do with—'

'She wanted us to sign a letter complaining about the noise issuing from one of the apartments.' He watched her freeze, then try very hard to hide her anxiety—a poker player this girl was not! 'Your apartment.' She gulped. 'I think she found Carlo's attitude perplexing. He couldn't understand why, if there were babies crying at all hours, she did not go and offer the mother her help. But then British restaurants which ban children are equally a mystery to him. Italian culture does not discriminate in this way,' he explained. 'Children are considered a gift, not something adults need to be shielded from.'

Whilst he had raised some very interesting points on cultural differences, Jude's attention was not at that moment concentrated on the British attitude to children. She was totally humiliated. She'd bounced in, oozing moral superiority, so sure—so very sure—that Luca was the person responsible.

Of course, now it was too late she recognised that if she had actually stopped and thought, not leapt in with guns blazing, she would have realised that the time-scale didn't fit the facts. She had only met Luca two days before, whereas the younger of the two women had revealed that they had received the complaint several days earlier. To add insult to injury, she recalled that the horrid Mrs Montgomery had been involved in a similar dispute with another neighbour.

But she hadn't stopped or thought, which was why she was standing here with egg all over her face struggling to say sorry to the one person in the world she least wanted to grovel to.

'Mrs Montgomery reported the tenants in one of the ground-floor flats when they had a puppy—there was a clause in their lease,' she recounted unhappily.

'That seems in character.'

'Then it really wasn't you who reported me?' she whispered.

'I'm sorry, but no.'

Jude groaned.

'I have to assume that Mrs Montgomery didn't canvass the support she needed and chose an alternative course of action.'

'Oh, God!' She took a deep breath and lifted her chin. 'I suppose I owe you an apology,' she admitted grudgingly.

'Marry me and we will call it quits.'

A startled hiss was drawn from her throat as Jude's wide eyes meshed with his. Two of the very last things she had expected to see were humour and warmth, but both were there in those dark, liquid depths. Suddenly she was more confused than ever. She shook her head and a shaky laugh was drawn from her tight, aching throat.

'Don't you ever give up?'

'No.' This time there was no humour in his eyes; instead she saw something that made her stomach dip violently.

'I know it's no excuse but I was scared,' she began to explain hurriedly in a broken voice. 'You know, at the thought of someone taking the children off me.'

Luca saw the luminous eyes she raised to his face were filled with very real horror.

'In fact, you would have done anything to stop that happening, wouldn't you, Jude?'

He was right. When did that happen? she wondered.

Luca continued to hold her eyes with a steady, questioning gaze.

'Oh!' she exclaimed, when the penny dropped. 'You're saying that's why you…that's the way *you* feel…?'

'We have finally discovered some common ground, it would seem.'

'A few days ago,' she admitted, 'I would have been grateful if someone had taken the responsibility off my shoulders.' Tears of shame stood out in her eyes as she bit down hard on her lower lip to stop it trembling. 'I know you probably don't think my feelings can compare with those of a biological parent…obviously I don't know what it feels like to be a mother, but I just can't imagine I could feel more for a child of my own.'

'Do not assume to read my mind or know my opinions.'

There was a note in his harsh intervention that brought her frowning attention to his face. His brooding expression did not further enlighten her and she was left with the vague feeling she had just missed something that was significant.

'I know you care for the children,' he added shortly. 'That is not the issue here.'

'I thought David was mad making me their legal guardian…mind you, there isn't anyone else, except Mum.' The intensity of his regard made her nervous. 'Correction,' she added with a laugh. 'There isn't anyone else…' Her eyes widened in alarm. 'Oh, God, I left the children with Mum. I should go…' She turned towards the door but Luca, who moved remarkably quickly for a man of his size, got there before her.

She faced him warily, her heart thudding like a sledgehammer against her breastbone. 'I really have to go…' To her dismay the words emerged minus the necessary ring of conviction. In fact, there was a troubling note that suggested she wouldn't mind someone persuading her to change her mind.

'Would it not be worth some…sacrifice on your part to ensure that there are never, ever any knocks on the door in future? That the children have a secure future…' He held up his hand. 'Do not insult me by pretending you have not thought about my proposition, Jude. Even when you were ridiculing it you were thinking about it. You are an intelligent woman—do not let your prejudices stand in the way of you making the right decision.'

'Marriage isn't meant to be a sacrifice.' She was relieved to hear herself sound almost normal.

It was hard to speak, when he stood between her and freedom. On previous occasions she'd experienced the way her brain shifted down a gear when she was close to him, but this time it was debilitating. As if to compensate for her lack of brain function her senses became more acute; it made for an uncomfortable combination.

Under normal circumstances she would probably have been blissfully unconscious of the male scent rising from his warm skin, but at that moment it filled her senses.

'Marriage is meant to be a great many things which it rarely, if ever, is, *cara*.'

The endearment, though she knew it had no significance, brought a lump to her throat. 'That's a very cynical thing to say.' Head tilted to one side in a questioning gesture he was beginning to recognise, she ran a finger across the arch of one feathery brow. 'Weren't you married to Valentina's mother?'

'I have never been married to anyone.'

'But did you want to be?'

'Please do not imagine me the victim of some ill-fated romance,' he commanded with a pained grimace.

'I wasn't.'

'You were,' he contradicted. 'I know what that misty look means on a female's face. Cloying sentimentality makes me queasy.'

'Thank you for sharing that with me. I'll try and remember in the future,' she promised. It was amazing, she reflected, that someone who looked so much like most women's idea of a romantic hero should actually be so totally and utterly unromantic.

'So you are finally admitting we have a future.'

'Your head is the only place we have a future.'

'I am not married for the simple reason I have never wanted to marry—until now, of course.'

'But you don't want to marry me...not *really*.' She scanned his handsome face worriedly in case he had detected the same wistful note her own ears had. Finding the most discernible expression on his face was mild irritation was actually quite a relief.

'What part of "will you marry me?" gives you that idea?'

'I'm an insurance policy.'

'Why do you keep throwing that casual remark back at me? You are a very beautiful woman,' he corrected, slick as silk.

Jude gave an angry snort; for a man who had had a lot of practice at saying the right thing to women that hadn't been very original. She had seen the sort of women he dated—did he really think she would imagine even for one second that he considered her anything more than average?

'Sure, I cause traffic jams when I walk down the street. And if I wasn't so *beautiful*, you wouldn't want to marry me, I suppose?'

'The fact you are is a plus point.'

Her curiosity wouldn't allow her to let the subject go. 'There must have been a few near misses marriage-wise.'

'No.'

'What are you—allergic to commitment? I mean, you're not exactly a spring chicken, are you?'

Luca blinked. 'I am thirty-two, if that is what you wanted to know. I still have all my own teeth.' He flashed them to prove the point. 'And my father still has a full head of hair, so genetically the odds are in my favour of keeping mine. I don't know if any of this influences your decision.'

'It doesn't.'

'There has never been any incentive before for me to get married. I already have a child, which is about the only possible reason I can see for marriage.'

'Love?' she protested, then blushed as his sensual lips formed a smile. She looked away from his dark, mocking eyes.

'*Love* is little more than temporary chemical imbalance. And marriage is based on the concept that that imbalance will last a lifetime.' He released a scornful laugh. 'You think, *cara*, because your heart beats a little faster when I am close to you that you love me? It is not love, it is sex that quickens the breath.' His dark lashes swept downwards as his attention moved to the outline of her heaving breasts. 'And raises the temperature.'

Jude placed a protective hand over her wildly thudding

heart and shook her head. 'It doesn't!' she denied. 'I'm not,' she added in a shaky whisper.

'Of course it does, as does mine,' he rasped thickly. 'Do not go coy on me. I admired your honesty last night.'

'I wasn't myself last night,' she insisted as he moved towards her. 'I didn't mean a word of it…'

'Yes, you did, and so did I. I find you attractive—is this such a difficult concept for you to grasp?' he demanded.

Jude shook her head and covered her ears with her hands. 'I don't believe you,' she cried. 'You're just trying to confuse me.' And succeeding fairly spectacularly!

She was too shocked to resist when he caught hold of her wrist, white-hot heat like lightning zigzagged through her body from the point of contact. As she dazedly focused on his face he twined his brown fingers into hers and, pushing aside his robe, placed her fingers against the warm skin of his chest. Her nostrils quivered as she inhaled sharply in shock.

'No!' Her chest rose and fell rapidly in agitation as she desperately tried to pull away.

'You told me you want me.'

She closed her eyes and groaned. Was she *ever* going to live that down?

'But even if you hadn't, do you think I don't know when a woman wants me?' He traced the outline of her jaw with the tip of one finger. He smiled when she shivered. 'Jude?'

'I don't! This is s…self-delusion.' His or mine?

'The only person deluding themselves here is you.' He responded as if he'd read her thoughts. 'You're holding back from what you know is a practical and workable solution to both our problems,' he condemned.

If he carried on believing that was all she was holding back, she could live with it. She didn't want to contemplate the humiliation of his knowing her true feelings.

'And why? Because you're waiting for some romantic love that simply doesn't exist outside the pages of romantic fiction.' His expressive lips thinned in distaste. 'You've got to face facts.'

'Your facts!' she cried.

'I'm sorry to be brutal, but—'

'No, you're not sorry!' she cut in angrily. 'You *enjoy* making fun of people's dreams.'

'Don't be stupid.'

'Disagreeing with you doesn't automatically make someone stupid, Luca. You haven't got any dreams left and you don't want anyone else to have them either!' she accused.

A muscle clenched in his lean cheek as his flinty eyes locked down onto hers. She felt dizzy but was unable to break the mesmeric contact. It seemed to her feverish imagination that she could actually see smoking embers in the dark, velvety depths of his dark-lashed eyes.

'So what does this man you dream of have that I don't, *cara*? Does he have blond hair and blue eyes, the studious spectacles, perhaps, that indicate his deeply *sensitive* nature? Will he quote Shakespeare's sonnets by way of foreplay, or do you prefer someone who can mend fuses and bring you tea in bed?'

His savage sarcasm made her flinch. 'I can mend my own fuses and it's not important what he looks like.'

'Of course it's not,' he agreed. 'That's because you're going to fall in love with his beautiful soul. *Dio!* But I'm all choked up just thinking about it.' As he spoke he could feel the small hand he held within his tighten into a fist. 'I suppose it's your extreme indifference to something as trivial as looks that has had your eyes all over me like a rash? And it wouldn't bother you if I took this off…' he suggested, unpicking the loose knot on the cord of his robe.

'Don't you dare!' She gasped in horror. '*Please*, Luca.' She heaved a sigh of relief when his hand fell away. 'Are you happy now you've proved how damned irresistible you are?' she choked. 'Your problem—' she began, only to be interrupted by a staccato burst of his hoarse, incredulous laughter.

'*I* have a problem? Yes,' he agreed, his eyes raking contemptuously over her face, 'I do—*you*! My God, you are the most infuriating woman I have ever met!'

The pent-up breath escaped in a long hiss through her clenched teeth. 'You want to know who my ideal lover would be? Well, not you would be good to be going on with,' she declared, her eyes spitting fury. 'You have to be the most joyless person I've ever come across and that includes the ones who were suffering from clinical depression! Don't you ever *dream*?'

This time his eyes held no smoking embers but a conflagration. When she gave a scared little gasp and tried to look away he took hold of her chin between his thumb and forefinger and tilted her face up to him.

'I have dreams, but I don't think you're ready to share them just yet.' His voice, low and fascinatingly accented, had a hypnotic quality; it suggested exciting, forbidden things that sent an illicit shudder through her body.

'The state of your sordid subconscious is of no interest whatever to me.'

'I think it interests you greatly.'

'Well, you think wrong.' Her defiance disintegrated when he suddenly leaned down towards her until his mouth was on a level with hers. She felt the warmth of his breath on her skin.

'You tremble when I touch you,' he purred complacently.

Wave after wave of wanting rolled over her as she stared hopelessly into his incredible face. Her breathing slowed down to nothing, she was paralysed with lust, every muscle, every fibre of her body, each individual brain cell frozen in anticipation of his kiss.

His dark head bent lower and her eyes closed and then she heard him murmur.

'Could your ideal lover do that?'

It took a second for the mocking words to penetrate the sensual fog she was drowning in; when they finally did she stiffened.

'You bastard!' she cried.

Burning with mortification, she tried to turn her face away from his mocking gaze, but he held her fast. She closed her eyes but it didn't shut out the image of his face. In her head she could see his dark, compelling eyes burning through the delicate paper-thin flesh on her eyelids.

Slowly her fingers unfurled and her eyes flickered open. Like someone suffering from tunnel vision, all she could see was his face.

'I can't take my eyes off you,' she confessed in a driven, confused voice. 'You know that.' Tiny fractured gasps emerged from her lips as she tentatively began to stretch her fingertips until her hand lay palm down against his skin.

Something fierce and primal flared in Luca's proud, strong boned face. 'That's it, *cara*,' he sighed with husky approval as he released her hand.

She felt the shudder that vibrated through his body.

'You feel it. You feel my heart beat for you.'

'For me?' she said in a small voice.

He nodded. 'You are so beautiful.'

'You don't have to say that,' she replied, most of her mind concentrated on the heavy thud of his heart under her fingertips. His flesh was warm and hard with a texture like oiled silk—the intimacy was intoxicating. Her throat ached with emotions, her body light and strangely unconnected; she was floating.

'I *want* to say that.' He took her other hand and raised it to his mouth. Almost reverently he pressed his lips to the palm. 'Such a little hand,' he rasped in the sexy accented drawl that never failed to send a secret thrill through her. 'The chemistry, it has been there since the first moment you glared at me with those beautiful, hungry eyes.'

He bent his head and kissed the pulse spot at the base of her neck. Jude's head fell back, exposing the long, lovely line of her throat in an unconsciously submissive gesture to him.

It was when he wound his fingers into her hair that Jude lifted her head. Her eyes were half closed as she looked at him with slumberous longing.

'You think you can make me agree to anything if you take me to bed,' she accused.

His bold eyes laughed confidently down into hers. 'Only in the short term, *cara mia*. A priest would not approve of the groom making love to his bride at the altar.'

'Even if I *do* sleep with you it doesn't mean I'm going to marry you.'

'You do not have the personality of a mistress.'

'Well, I bow to your superior knowledge of the subject.'

'Before you start introducing conditions again, perhaps,' he suggested huskily, 'you should consider that two can play at that game.' Smiling fiercely down into at her bewildered face, he elaborated. 'I could for instance say if you won't marry me I won't make love to you.'

Every nerve in her body screamed out in protest at the suggestion.

'You're not serious!' She scanned his face for any sign this was an empty threat and found none. It was a very persuasive argument.

With a throaty murmur in his native tongue he suddenly

pulled her close, crushing her soft body to him. 'Does this feel as if I have that sort of control?' he demanded roughly.

The bewilderment in her eyes was swallowed up by an expression of simmering sexual awareness when, placing a hand in the small of her back, Luca pressed her even harder against his lean body. His fingers splayed into the hollow at the base of her spine, effectively sealing their bodies together at hip level.

The thin robe he wore did little to disguise what was happening to his body. Feeling his arousal grinding into the softness of her belly drove the last rational thought from Jude's head. Eyes closed, lips parted, she squirmed ecstatically up against him and gasped as she felt his powerful body pulse in response.

'Do I feel like I could play hard to get?' he tormented softly.

Jude, weak with hunger for him, sobbed his name.

Luca scanned her face hungrily before expertly parting her trembling lips and sinking into her mouth with a deep groan. He did not kiss her gently, but tore at her lips frantically with a bruising hunger. Jude's response to the stabbing incursions of his tongue was equally wild and out of control.

'*Dio*, but that mouth,' he slurred thickly when they finally broke apart. His hot eyes ate up the delicate details of the flushed features turned up to him. Something primal buried deep inside her responded to the sexual challenge she saw blazing in the spectacular eyes of his.

In an unconsciously sultry manner she looked down and then allowed her slumberous gaze to travel up to his face. 'What about my mouth?' she asked innocently.

'It is made for kissing. Just as you are made for loving— for loving me,' he added, sliding his hand under her sweater and up across her narrow ribcage.

Her startled body jerked as the contact sent an electric thrill shooting all the way down to her curling toes.

From where Luca stood he could not see her eyes, just the

heavy sweep of her lashes lying against the curve of her cheekbones. The tips he saw were pure gold. Her skin was milk-pale barring the thin ribbons of feverish colour slashed across her soft cheeks. The pupils of his eyes responded to the image of a deeply aroused woman and dramatically expanded until only a thin rim of iris remained visible.

As his fingers rubbed across the tight peak of the soft, warm flesh it pushed through the stretchy fabric that restrained it.

'I need to see you,' he told her thickly as he urgently peeled the cotton top off her. Firmly he unfolded the arms she had pressed protectively across her chest.

Embarrassment overcame her. 'I wasn't expecting…this isn't very…' The sports bra she wore was hardly a garment designed with seduction in mind.

'If you wish me to remove lacy undergarments I will buy you some,' he promised. 'However, *I* do not require such stimulus. I just,' he explained, holding her eyes with his needy gaze, 'require you.'

Tears started in her eyes. 'Truly?' she whispered.

'Absolutely.' Still holding her eyes with his own, he released the front fastening on her bra. His glance dropped as the fabric parted. 'You are perfect,' he gasped raggedly in a voice approaching reverence as his scorching gaze took in every aspect of the heaving, pink-tipped mounds of firm, soft flesh.

Jude moaned as he took one tingling mound, weighing it in his palm. His thumb rubbed across the engorged nipple, sending sharp currents of tingling sensation jolting through her body.

'See how well you fill my hand.' Luca shared the deep, primal satisfaction on discovering that her straining breast fitted so perfectly into his palm.

A soft, sibilant hiss escaped her parted lips as her head, too heavy now for her neck to support, fell bonelessly back. As it did so he twisted the loose curls that spilled back from her face into his fist. Then as it fell forward against his chest his hand moved to cup the back of her head.

'Oh, God, Luca, I didn't know it could be like this…'

He bent his head to her ear. 'And you like this?'

'Like?' She groaned and lifted her head. His dark eyes drew her restless gaze like a magnet. 'God, I love it…' I love you, she thought.

If she didn't tell him about her brilliant idea now she might never get around to it. 'Luca…?'

'Mmm…?'

'Have you thought that maybe we could just *pretend* we're married,' she suggested inventively.

She felt his body stiffen.

'No, I haven't.' His tone did not invite further discussion. *'Pretending* is not part of the bargain, but this,' he promised thickly, 'is.' Without warning he scooped her up into his arms and, carrying her over to the bed, lowered her onto the silk cover.

For a moment he stood just looking at her. The throbbing, expectant silence filled Jude's head like a drum beat. She actually read Luca's intention in the glittering challenge of his eyes about a split second before he began to loosen the belt on his robe.

She lay there dry-mouthed with anticipation as he shrugged it off. The sight of him standing looking like a magnificent statue of male perfection would have moved the most dispassionate of onlookers to awe. Jude felt as if her heart were in a vice.

It was remarkable to her that—for whatever reason—he wanted her. Of course, she knew *wanting* for a man was easy, but at that moment it was enough for her that he did.

Jude heard with a sense of detached disbelief the raw moan of longing that emerged from her bone-dry throat.

The sound made his smoky eyes blaze in male triumph and

his already primed male body react in a way that made her gasp. She tried to imagine him moving inside her, picturing his bronzed body pressing down on her, the weight of his limbs pinning her…but stopped because the distant buzzing in her ears got noisily close and shoals of red dots had started to drift across her vision thickened to a thin red mist. Could a person faint from lust?

I could be the first. Well, this is a day for firsts.

Her inability to take her greedy eyes off him made Luca laugh and plead only half jokingly, 'If you look at me like that, *cara*, this thing might be over before it has begun.'

When the implication of his earthy observation penetrated her dazed condition a fresh flush of heat seeped through her already burning body. She shivered voluptuously when he leaned down to run his tongue along the valley between her bare rosy-tipped breasts. Lifting his head, he took her hands between his and ran the tip of his tongue along the moist edge of her parted lips. She wanted to feel his tongue inside her mouth, but none of her frantic, fractured pleas made him kiss her properly.

'Oh, God, Luca!' she panted in frustration when he drew back. 'I'll die if you don't kiss me!' she claimed with total conviction.

'Slowly,' he soothed, raking an unsteady hand through his sweat-dampened hair. 'I want this to be special. I want you to remember this.'

The idea that there was even the remotest possibility of her forgetting this brought a strained smile to her lips. 'Forgettable isn't the first word that springs to mind when I look at you.'

'Tell me what word springs to your mind when you look at me,' he suggested as he placed his hands either side of her shoulders.

'I don't want to talk,' she said as he lowered himself down

beside her—*finally*! She thought his soft laughter was pretty callous considering how she was hurting and might have told him so had he not chosen that moment to adjust her body so that they were lying side by side…thigh to thigh.

'What do you want to do?'

The light brush of his velvet hard erection against the waistband of her jeans sent a visible ripple of movement across her abdomen as the fine muscles beneath the skin contracted. Deeper inside everything just melted.

'You're very good at this, aren't you?' she whispered, looking deep into his eyes, eyes so dark and warm you could lose yourself in them.

'Would that be a bad thing?'

It might be if I turn out to be not so good at it. She was all right on the theory, but would she be able to put it into practice?

Luca, who had been trying as hard as he could to ignore the uneasy vibes he was picking up from her, found that he couldn't.

Jude was alarmed when without warning he rolled onto his back and lay there with his crooked arm over his eyes. God, did I do something? Did I not do something…?

'Are you all right with this?' He held his breath. If she said no he didn't know what the hell he'd do because the five-miles run and cold showers he'd been taking on what seemed an hourly basis since he had first met this woman were not going to work today. There was only so far a man could run!

Jude found herself wishing she taken up some of the offers of meaningless sex she'd turned down over the years. Then she looked into his eyes and thought, No, I'm glad I didn't. This is going to be something special, something worth waiting for.

'I'm fine with this,' she announced firmly.

He rolled back in time to be on the receiving end of a sultry smile that made him just want to rip off her remaining clothes and to bury himself in her.

'Why don't you make up your own mind about me?' he suggested, curving a big hand possessively around her left breast. 'You like that?' he said, his voice thick with satisfaction as she moaned. When he ran his tongue wetly across one brazenly erect nipple her back arched and she cried out.

'Yes, I like it!'

When his lips and teeth continued the tormenting, teasing over her sensitised flesh, she lost what little control she had retained over what came out of her mouth.

'I've wanted you to do this for ever. I wanted you to do this from the moment...oh, God, I wanted you to do this *before* I even saw you!' A sigh was wrenched from somewhere incredibly deep down inside her. 'I just want you, Luca.'

His head lifted. 'Then take me, *cara mia.*'

She laid her hands against the warm skin of his shoulders. It felt smooth like oiled silk and the male scent of him was addictive—*he* was addictive. It was at that point sanity took a back seat. For several minutes they kissed and touched in a desperate, almost combative fashion.

There were two slashes of dark colour along Luca's cheekbones, nail marks on his shoulders and a feverish glow in his eyes when they finally broke for air.

'Perhaps I should have said earlier—assertive women scare me,' he explained in between gasps. 'I feel threatened.'

'You don't look threatened.' Part of her registered that he was shaking just as hard as she was. She brought her lips to the strong column of his brown throat and pressed a series of open-mouthed kisses to his damp flesh.

'How do I look?'

She angled her head so that she could see his face and holding his eyes, allowed her tongue to flick across his salty skin. *'Perfect.'*

He groaned something in Italian and continued to speak the

same language in a deep, driven voice as he slid his long fingers under the waistband of her jeans. Her body tensed expectantly. His quest towards the moist heat was prevented by the constriction of her clothes.

There was no longer any pretence of controlling the pace about Luca's actions as he ripped urgently at the zip of her jeans. It gave way and he parted the thick fabric, revealing the thin lacy covering through which the soft fuzz of hair at the apex of her smooth thighs was visible.

Despite the fact that the strong hands that tugged her jeans down over her hips and legs were not quite steady, it only took a few seconds for Jude to be divested of everything but the tiny triangle of lace. His fingers slid under the insubstantial barrier.

For a split second her body tensed at the shocking intimacy of his touch, then as he began to stroke her she relaxed and was lost to everything but what was happening to her—what Luca was making happen. She barely even registered him sliding the damp lace down her thighs. Every cell in her body was screaming out for release by the time he settled between her smooth thighs.

The husky words that emerged in staccato bursts from his lips as he parted her thighs were an incoherent mixture of English and Italian, but the extreme urgency of his actions and the ferocious, raw tension on his strained face did not need translation.

'You're mine!' he breathed into her ear in the split second before he thrust powerfully into her. *'Madre di Dio!'* He froze.

Beneath him Jude hardly registered his shocked cry. She had too much else to concentrate on, such as the overwhelming and totally amazing sensation of feeling the hard, hot length of him inside her. Her eyelids lifted from her feverishly flushed cheek.

She gave a tiny triumphant smile. 'I knew you'd be good.'

'This isn't good,' he breathed back.

Jude opened her mouth to contradict him when he began to move slowly…again and again, sinking deeper inside her, and she was lost to everything but him and the incredible pleasure and the pressure building up inside her. Her teeth closed around his shoulder when the shattering climax hit her, convulsing every cell in her body with intense pleasure. Only then did she hear his hoarse cry and the pulsing heat of his release within her.

'*That* was good,' he sighed, slanting her a hot, complacent grin as he rolled off her.

Jude, who was panting almost as hard as he was, turned over onto her stomach and lifted a hand to his jaw. Her wondering eyes remained locked with his as she ran her fingers along his stubble-roughened lean cheek.

'That was *incredible*,' she corrected huskily. 'You were incredible.'

His dark head turned sideways on the pillow. 'I'm your first lover.'

Warily she nodded. 'Yes.'

'This was a…?'

'Listen, it just never happened, *all right*?' she challenged fiercely. 'I do not have any major hang-ups, I was not waiting for Mr Right, it just never happened, end of story!' With a final glare at him she rolled away from him.

'Do not turn your back on me!' he yelled, grabbing her shoulder and rolling her back to him.

'I'll do anything I damn well—'

A muscle in his lean cheek jerked. 'I could have hurt you.' The strong muscles in his throat worked as he swallowed. 'I wouldn't have…'

Jude's anger melted in the face of his concern, she touched a finger to his lips. 'You didn't hurt me, Luca, and you were perfect.'

For a long moment his eyes searched her face. 'I think you should marry me.'

There was something quite liberating about running out of options—you didn't have to make a decision, it made itself. Well, if that's your story, girl, stick to it like glue, the voice in her head advised drily.

'I think so too,' she agreed quietly.

Luca, who obviously possessed remarkable appetites and recuperative powers to match, decided they were already in the perfect place to celebrate their engagement.

Some time later she lay wrapped in both Luca's arms and the contented afterglow of his lovemaking.

'This wasn't what I planned today,' she murmured with a smile as he swept the tumble of curls from her face to kiss her damp forehead.

'What did you plan?'

'I was going to take the…oh, my God, the children! *Mum!*' She shot out of bed and began running around the room in a frenzied effort to locate her discarded clothing.

'If the children are with your mother, surely there is no problem,' Luca mused, a hand tucked behind his head as he watched with an expression of amusement her frantic and clumsy efforts to fight her way into her clothes.

'You,' she told him darkly, 'have never met my mother.'

Luca had risen in a more leisurely fashion from the bed and pulled on his robe by the time she had finished dressing. It occurred to her as she walked to the door that, other than agreeing to marry, they had discussed very little of the practicalities.

She paused, her hand on the door handle. 'I was wondering if you'd thought about when we might actually…' she gave an awkward grimace '…you know, *do* it. I suppose there's quite a lot to sort out.' At least that would give her some time to prepare the children, not to mention herself.

'Saturday.'

Jude's jaw dropped. 'Saturday! You've got to be joking.' Suddenly this thing was running away, and she was losing control of the direction it was taking. You lost control the moment you met him, she reminded herself.

'Leave me to organise the children's passports. I assume that yours is up to date.'

'Of course it is, but what do I need a passport for? It's not like we'll be taking a honeymoon.'

'We'll be getting married at the chapel in my family home.'

'Italy!' she gasped.

He looked mildly amused by her open-mouthed astonishment. 'And we will be taking a honeymoon,' he added in a non-negotiable tone. 'Nothing about this wedding is to give anyone reason to think it is a marriage of convenience. *Nothing…*' he repeated, just in case she hadn't already picked up on the fact he meant what he said.

The enormity of the deceit they were undertaking hit her afresh. Luca could close the door on the rest of the world and drop the act; she didn't have that luxury, because she had to keep up the pretence in front of him too!

If she let her guard down he would guess that she had fallen in love with him, and that was clearly not part of the bargain as far as he was concerned. Jude exhaled gustily before lifted her apprehensive eyes to his. 'I don't think I can do this.'

'Nonsense.' Luca dismissed her fears with a shrug and the sort of high-handed attitude she had come to expect of him.

'People will know.'

'People will know what we want them to and see what we allow them. Think of it this way—all you have to do is act like you are fighting a constant, but losing battle to keep your hands off me.' A slow, intimate smile that made her stomach muscles quiver curved his lips as his dark eyes scanned her flushed face. 'It's what you might call a role you were born for,' he added softly.

'The next thing you'll be telling me I was born for you,' she slung over her shoulder as she walked out of the door.

CHAPTER NINE

LYN Lucas pushed her aching feet back into her four-inch stilettos at the sound of the door opening. 'Do you know what time it is?' she demanded, her normally beautifully modulated voice shrill. After flicking off the switch on the television she rose to her feet, smoothing down a crease in her skirt as she turned around.

'I came here to see you and what do you do? Disappear without a word. I call that thoughtless and inconsiderate. I had absolutely no idea where you were. The children wanted their supper and baths…' she related with an expressive little shudder. 'Have you *any* idea how exhausting it is to…?' She stopped, catching sight of her daughter's expression. 'What's happened to you?'

'I think…' A wash of soft colour tinged Jude's pale skin as she lifted her chin. 'No, I *know*,' she corrected firmly.

'Do you mind sharing what you "know"?'

'I just got engaged.'

'*Engaged?*' Lyn scanned her daughter's softly flushed face suspiciously. 'Have you been drinking, Jude?'

'No, but I think I might start.'

'Good God!' Lyn gasped. 'You're serious, aren't you? How could you get engaged dressed like that?' Her critical gaze slid over her casually dressed daughter. 'And your hair—having children is no excuse to let yourself go. Does he know about the children? No, I don't suppose he does.'

'Yes, he knows about the children, Mum.'

'What does he do? And is he solvent, Jude? Oh, I know you'll say that money doesn't matter, but believe me it helps.'

'You can relax, Mum, he's financially secure. He's definitely not after my money.'

This information did not have the desired calming effect on her mother, who went deathly pale.

'Oh, God! This is *exactly* what I was afraid of…'

'What were you afraid of?' Jude asked, bewildered at this new tangent.

'You still think that if I hadn't divorced your father your childhood would have been so much rosier, don't you? Well, it wouldn't,' she rebutted bluntly. 'But we're not talking about my divorce here…'

'What are we talking about, Mum?'

'We're talking about you getting involved with some loser just to give the children financial security and a father-figure.'

There was *just* enough truth in this claim to make Jude look uncomfortable. Luca was the least 'loserish' man on the planet and she was madly in love with him, but there was no escaping the fact that they wouldn't be getting married if he hadn't needed a wife of convenience.

Lyn saw the guilty downward flicker of her daughter's eyes and clapped her hands over her mouth. 'I blame myself!' she announced dramatically.

Typical, after twenty-seven years my mum chooses to turn perceptive.

'I could tell you were desperate when you called me… I was too tough with you on the phone, I'm the first to admit it. That's why I had to come. I haven't been able to get the sound of your frantic voice out of my mind.'

'Mum…Mum, calm down!' Jude begged her distraught parent.

'I thought I'd taught you how important it is to retain your financial independence. Relationships are temporary; your bank balance, Jude,' she told her daughter heavily, 'is for life.'

Jude struggled to retain her composure. In her own rather unique way her mum was clearly trying to look out for her daughter's best interests.

'Which is why,' Lyn continued, 'I've been discussing the matter with my accountant.'

'Your accountant?' Jude echoed, lost again.

'Yes, and according to him I might just as well give you the money that's going to come to you when I die now, when you genuinely need it.'

'Mum!' Jude cried, genuinely touched by this unexpected gesture from her normally less-than-open-handed parent. A tough, impoverished childhood, which she rarely spoke of, had made Lyn Lucas extremely careful with her money, and fearful of losing her financial security.

'It's not a lot, so don't get excited. So you see you don't need to settle for second best. Your problem is you don't believe in yourself…and what you have to offer. You're a clever, beautiful young woman, but if you don't rate yourself nobody else will, Jude.'

Jude went forward and threw her arms around her mother. 'That's the sweetest thing you've ever said to me,' she told her, planting a kiss on her mother's smooth cheek.

'Yes, well…' Lyn murmured, looking shaken but pleased as she emerged from the spontaneous embrace. 'There's no need to go overboard—it's not that much money,' she said gruffly.

'I'm just thanking you for caring,' Jude said with a watery smile. 'I don't want your money.'

'You're not still marrying this loser? I forbid it, Jude.'

'Mum, he's not a loser and he's *definitely* not second best.' The notion of Luca, who didn't have a word for lose in his vocabulary, being second *anything* was so absurd it was hard not to laugh out loud.

'I am most relieved to hear you say so, *cara*.'

Both women gasped in unison and spun in the direction of the deep, throaty drawl.

'What are you doing here?' Jude demanded, her face burning with embarrassed colour.

One dark brow adopted the satirical slant she was growing to know so well. 'I thought you might be missing me,' he suggested with an air of very unconvincing innocence.

'There's no need to look so unbearably smug,' she told the tall, vital figure who sent her pulse rate soaring. 'I was about to qualify my observation with what you *are*.'

'*Are* as in charming, adorable, incredibly intelligent?'

'*Are* as in infuriating, bossy, and overbearing.'

He grinned at her tart retort.

Lyn Lucas, who had been watching this interchange with slack-jawed astonishment, closed her mouth with an audible click and cleared her throat. 'Jude, are you going to introduce me to…?' As she spoke her eyes didn't stray from the tall, supremely elegant figure. 'My goodness,' she gasped with a laugh, 'you look just like—'

Jude cut in quickly. 'Mum, this is Luca. Luca Di Rossi.' Luca obligingly placed a hand on her shoulder and a faint choking sound emerged from her mother's open mouth.

'You're going to marry Luca Di Rossi.' Her mother's beautifully modulated voice was an incredulous squeak. 'Gianluca Di Rossi? This isn't a joke?'

Her mother's stupefaction was hardly flattering, but Jude could well understand it.

'It's no joke, Mum. Luca, this is my mother, Lyn Lucas.

Mum, I'm *really* sorry to dump on you like that, I didn't intend to be so long.' She felt a guilty flush mount her cheeks.

'Do not blush, *cara*, your mother knows what it is like to lose track of time when you are with your future husband.' His enquiring glance slid to the older woman.

'What? Oh, yes, of course I do…' Lyn responded faintly.

'I'm afraid I'm the one to blame. I have so little opportunity to have Jude to myself it makes me selfish.'

As he spoke her name their eyes brushed and a tingling sensation passed through Jude's body, which still ached in a pleasurable way from their recent lovemaking. Of course, he was playing a part for the benefit of her mother, but it didn't make her own responses any less real.

He reached out and lifted a soft tendril of hair off her cheek. Jude flinched and apologised profusely as she stepped backwards and trod on his foot.

'I hope I didn't hurt you.' Under the cover of apologising she whispered. *'Go away!'*

'You didn't hurt me, *cara*. You have such delicate little feet. Mrs Lucas, I'm so glad I have the opportunity of meeting you at last. It's so good of you to give Jude a break this way. We both know that she's too stubborn to ask for help even when she needs it.'

'Oh, that's *so* true and she's always been that way even when she was a child.'

'I *hate* to interrupt but,' Jude interrupted sarcastically, 'in case you didn't notice, *I'm* here!'

'And so am I,' added her mother emotionally. 'I'm here for you whenever you need me, darling.'

Of course it was possible her mother had been replaced by an alien, but it was much more likely that this earth-mother role had something to do with a desire to impress Luca with her empathy. Jude almost immediately felt ashamed of her uncharitable thought. The fact that she was here proved that she did care.

'I think the likelihood of any of us forgetting that you are here is remote.' Luca looked away and exchanged a conspiratorial look with her mother, who was almost visibly falling under his spell.

'So how long have you two known one another?'

'With some people you can know them all your life and never really know them at all…with others…' His gleaming jet eyes stroked suggestively over Jude's face. 'Others,' he sighed and gave an expressive shrug. 'A second is enough to tell you all you need to know.'

Jude wondered if her mother, whose eyes had misted over as he'd spoken, would even notice that he hadn't answered her question.

'That's so true!' Lyn sighed.

'Oh, *please*!'

Luca slipped an arm around her waist. 'Did you say something, *cara mia*?'

Lyn, watching them, sighed. 'What a lovely couple you make, though if you'd been blonde, Jude…' she mused, her eyes touching her daughter's dark brown hair regretfully. 'But not to worry. Have you set a date yet?'

'Saturday,' Luca supplied casually.

After the initial shock had worn off, Lyn went into full organisation mode, giving Luca lists of things that would need to be organised. Halfway through a discussion about the number of guests who would be able to attend at such short notice, she turned to her daughter.

'Why don't you go and make us a nice cup of tea, dear? Now, Luca…'

Jude was waiting for the kettle to boil when Luca walked in.

'What's wrong?' he asked, leaning against the wall as she brushed past him.

Jude set the carton of milk down with a bang. 'Nothing.'

'I hate women who sulk,' he observed, sounding bored.

'Sulk?' She swung around, her eyes flashing. 'This is meant to be *my* wedding, isn't it?' One dark sardonic brow lifted in response to her bitter query.

'Oh, I know it's not a *proper* wedding, but it would be nice,' she quivered, swallowing past the emotional lump in her throat, 'if I had *some* say in it. Actually I doubt if anyone would notice if I actually didn't turn up.'

'I would notice.'

Her wilful heart flipped at this soft interruption.

'You would?' She sniffed and raised her eyes to his. 'Well, of course you would, you need me.'

'I need you,' he echoed in agreement.

'For Valentina,' she added.

His wide, mobile lips formed a twisted smile. 'What other reason could there be, *cara*?'

Jude had finished her packing the night before. Her mother, who was still utterly intoxicated by the realisation her only daughter had netted the matrimonial catch of the century, had offered in a fit of grandmotherly fervour to take the children to the zoo to give her 'a bit of quality time, darling' before the flight.

'You're going to have the eyes of the world on you,' she announced portentously to her already nervous daughter, 'so you'll need to look your best.'

'Is that meant to relax me? Because I have to tell you—'

'Whatever made you think weddings were meant to be re-laxing for a woman?' She laughed out loud at the notion, but almost immediately sobered. 'The fact is you owe it to Luca. I mean, you only have to think about the women he's used to being around. A man like that expects a certain sort of standard.'

'Actually, Mum, I'm trying to forget the sort of women he dates.' If this maternal pep talk went on much longer she might just lose the will to live.

'What's this—a crisis of confidence?'

'What, with you around to bolster my ego?'

Jude's gentle irony went right over her mother's head. 'I'm here to help,' she agreed. 'But when you have doubts just remember: he chose you, not them…' A mystified expression entered her eyes as she shook her head.

Of course, she didn't know the real reason for the rush marriage so Luca's preference for a short, average-looking brunette was something her mum still couldn't quite get her head around, but then, Jude reflected ruefully, she never had let motherly love blind her to hard facts.

One of Jude's earliest memories was being taken to an eighth birthday party by her mother and being told in a hushed aside as she had had the smudges wiped from her nose that it didn't matter if she wasn't the prettiest girl there, she could be the most interesting.

She could smile about it now. At the time it hadn't been so easy—eight-year-old girls did not much want to be interesting! On reflection it was actually pretty amazing that she hadn't ended up walking around with a brown paper bag over her head!

'Then wouldn't it be a bit silly for me to try and look like them—even,' she added drily, 'if it was possible.'

'Well, I dare say the novelty factor comes into it…but you can't expect that to last for ever.'

A genuine laugh was torn from Jude's throat. 'So what you're trying to tell me is the honeymoon's over before the wedding has taken place?'

'I'm telling you, child,' Lyn replied, irritated by her

daughter's refusal to take the matter seriously, 'that there's no harm making the best of what you have.'

It wasn't until after her mother had left that the real significance of this maternal remark became obvious, when in fact the entire staff—or so it seemed to Jude—of a well-known beauty establishment arrived on her doorstep armed to the teeth!

When they departed some two hours later Jude felt pretty much like a car that had gone through one of those automatic wax washes.

Her hair had been coaxed into its old pre-fizz sleekness. Her toenails and fingernails had acquired several coats of the latest shade of varnish, which, according to the manicurist, was so happening it was not going on sale to the general public until the autumn. Jude had dutifully expressed suitable gratitude and awe.

So here she was exfoliated, buffed and oiled until she was glowing. 'What now?' she demanded of the beautifully groomed frowning image in the mirror. 'Is this supposed to make him love me?' she mockingly continued. 'Oh, God, am I making the worst mistake of my life?' She was waiting in vain for the silent image to reply when she heard the sound of movement in the living room.

Assuming that one of the make-over team was still gathering their things, she tightened the belt on a fluffy towelling robe and padded through, barefoot, to the other room to chivvy them along.

'Did you forget something?' she began, then broke off. 'Marco!' she gasped as the blond-haired figure of Luca's sharply dressed younger half-brother was revealed.

Looking at him post-Luca, Jude could not help but compare him with his brother…it was automatic. Did people always do that to him? she wondered. It must be really terrible if they did. Did he mind living in the shadow of a brother who was *more* everything?

She asked the obvious question. 'What are you doing here?'

'I hope I didn't startle you. A guy with a hair-dryer let me in.'

'Blue hair?' He nodded. 'Ah, yes, that would be Rick. He said my hair was a challenge.'

'What a cheek. Well, I think it looks great.'

'Thank you,' she said, touching the bouncy bell of hair that swung around her face when she moved.

'If you're looking for Luca...' she felt herself colour and wondered if she was the only woman who felt awkward saying the name of the man she was going to marry '...he's not here... Well, he wouldn't be, we're not living together or anything.'

'No, you're just getting married.' His liquid brown eyes slid down her body admiringly. If Luca had done the same thing I'd have been toast, she thought, marvelling at the dramatic contrast to her response or, rather, lack of it when Marco employed one of his sultry Latin stares.

Marco sighed as his roaming gaze returned to her face. 'I had to see for myself it was true, and I see it is.' He nodded towards the square-cut emerald on her left hand.

'I suppose it seems a bit sudden.'

Marco grinned. 'Luca doesn't operate by the same rules as the rest of us. When he wants something he just goes for it, but then,' he added slyly, 'you already know that.'

His readiness to accept that Luca had fallen for her big time took Jude by surprise. She'd been geared up to face people's scepticism.

'It's been fast,' she agreed. 'I keep thinking I'm going to wake up,' she mused. 'I just can't decide yet whether it's a dream or a nightmare.'

Belatedly Jude became aware of Marco's startled expression. It was hardly surprising. Blushing brides-to-be didn't talk nightmares.

'The packing and organisation and everything—my feet haven't touched the ground yet,' she explained in an attempt to cover her slip.

To her relief it seemed to work, but she acknowledged she was going to have to watch her tongue in future. Luca would be furious if something she said made people suspicious about this marriage. It defeated the purpose of the marriage if anyone saw through the charade.

The problem was she was just so relaxed around Marco, relaxed in a way that she could never imagine being around Luca. If it had been Luca standing there, and she'd been in a similar state of partial dress, there wouldn't have been a single second she would not have been acutely conscious that underneath the robe she wore nothing.

Catching the lapels of her robe together in one hand, Jude pinned a bright smile on her face. 'Can I get you a coffee or anything?'

'A beer would be good, if you have one.'

Jude went over to the fridge and pulled out an iced bottle. 'This do?'

'Perfect.' He accepted with gratitude, took a swallow and sighed. 'I just thought I'd touch base with Luca on my way through.'

'Have you been away?'

Amusement appeared in his eyes. 'You didn't notice. You really know how to kick a man when he's down.'

'Well, of course I noticed you were away, and you know perfectly well there was never anything happening between us.'

Marco accepted her remonstrance with a grin. 'I guess there was something happening with Luca. You always were immune to my charms, but whilst you were unattached I could hope. I guess it's too late now. Don't worry,' he cut in, 'I'm not about to make a clumsy pass.'

'Good, because it would not only be embarrassing, but pointless,' she told him frankly.

'You're a cruel woman,' he complained, wincing. 'But you don't need to worry, I'm actually quite fond of my face the way it is.'

'I had noticed,' she inserted innocently.

Marco laughed. 'Well, being the vain, shallow creature I am I'd never, ever try to muscle in on my brother's territory— not even for my lovely little English rose,' he added gallantly.

'I'm sure Luca wouldn't do anything like that,' she protested.

'You don't think so? Well, you'll learn.'

Jude, who didn't like the sinister sound of that enigmatic observation, frowned.

'To be honest I usually get away with a rap on the knuckles, but he's never planned to marry any of them. Actually I'm be-ginning to suspect the real reason why I've spent the last week clocking up more air miles than...' He shrugged. 'Not that I'm complaining—I've always said I wanted more responsibility.'

'What do you mean?'

Marco shook his head cheerfully. 'Just thinking out loud. Apparently Luca's got an army at work getting everything ready for the big day. He really wants to pull out all the stops on this wedding and, like everyone else, I've had my list of must-do things. So when you see him—I'm assuming he won't be able to keep away for long—I thought not,' he added drily when Jude blushed. 'Tell my big brother it's all in hand and I'll see him tomorrow. Until then, how about a sisterly kiss?'

Laughing, Jude presented her dimpled cheek.

'I'd say I deserve more compensation than that,' he mur-mured, turning her chin and planting a warm kiss on her lips. The smile died from his face as he scanned her upturned features. 'It is just as well I am a shallow sort of guy, or it might take me a very long time to recover from this.'

A sudden volley of very furious Italian made Marco spring away from her as if he'd been shot.

Jude saw him close his eyes as if gathering his courage before he turned with a forced smile. 'Luca, I was hoping to catch you.'

His light-hearted tone didn't put a dent in his brother's stony expression. Luca's low response was in resonant Italian.

Jude, who heard her own name, found it deeply frustrating not be able to understand what was being said. Especially as whatever it was had such a conspicuous effect on Marco, who coloured deeply and began to shake his head. When he responded in the same language he sounded uneasy and his entire attitude was placatory. She wondered whether the brothers always acted this way or had perhaps had a recent falling-out.

The mystifying back-and-forth flow of words lasted a couple of minutes—minutes with Luca growing colder and Marco more subdued.

Finally Luca acknowledged her presence. Not before time, in her opinion.

His brows were drawn into a scowling line of disapproval as he scanned her face. 'What have you done to your hair?'

Jude blinked. 'I've had a make-over. Don't you like it?'

'No, I don't.'

She didn't cry because he didn't like her hair—that would have been just too pathetic. The fact that she *wanted to* filled her with despair. '*Marco* likes it.'

'*Marco* is just leaving,' Luca bit back without looking at his brother.

When he turned back to Jude, Marco's discomfort was obvious. 'I'm running late, I really have to be going. Thanks for the beer.'

Feeling for his embarrassment, Jude put some extra warmth into her smile to compensate for Luca's inexplicably hostile attitude. 'That's a pity. It's been really nice to catch up.' The defiant look she tossed at the tall, silent figure of her future husband shrivelled in face of the white-hot fury she encountered etched in the taut lines of his strong-boned face.

What on earth had Marco done to make him look like that? she wondered, pretty shaken by the dark brooding danger she had seen glittering in his incredible eyes. Well, she decided with a rebellious toss of her despised hair, whatever it was she damn well wasn't going to take the flak for it!

The moment he had gone Jude turned on Luca, her eyes flashing. 'What on earth did you say to him?' she demanded.

Luca, his shoulders pressed against the wall, continued to examine the toe of his handmade leather shoe as if it were more interesting than anything she might have to say. His indolent pose infuriated her even more.

'The poor thing looked really shaken,' she condemned. 'Everybody knows you're the boss…for heaven's sake, you never let us forget it! So is it really necessary to throw your weight around that way? Would it cost you anything to show a little bit of consideration?'

With an abrupt movement that startled her, Luca levered his lean body from the wall, drawing himself to his full and impressive height.

'*Consideration?*' His lashes lifted and Jude found the stormy expression glowing in those stunning depths did not mesh one little bit with his soft, conversational tone. Oh, my God! She was wrong, he wasn't angry—he was *incandescent*!

'You were very rude,' she said with slightly less conviction.

'I heard your laughter from halfway up the stairs.' She had never laughed that way with him. Luca fought to contain the fresh lick of anger that surged through his veins. 'I walk in and find my brother drooling over my bride, who is flaunting her body…'

Rather unfortunately, this unexpected and ludicrous explanation for his mood drew a startled laugh from her.

Luca drew a harsh breath. 'You find this amusing… You think it is a joke to behave like a tart?'

'*Tart!*' she gasped in hot-cheeked protest as his smouldering gaze lashed over her.

'Well, are you going to tell me you've got anything on under that thing?' demanded Luca, who had begun to pace up and down in front of her like a panther with attitude.

Jude's eyes widened in indignant protest. Anyone would think from the way he was talking that she were parading around in a sexy G-string and nothing else, instead of an androgynous robe that was as revealing as a tent. 'No,' she admitted, 'but—'

'But *nothing*!' he rapped, coming to a halt directly in front of her. 'I can see you have nothing on, do you think that Marco could not? Or maybe you had less on a little while earlier.' His eyes slitted suspiciously. 'Just how long has he been here?'

Jude went rigid with shock at this preposterous suggestion. It took every ounce of her self-control not to hit him.

'If you actually believe that I would jump into bed with your brother the moment your back is turned I think we'd better forget about this marriage.'

A visible shudder ran through his lean frame as he closed his eyes and rubbed an unsteady hand over his chin. 'No, I don't actually think that,' he admitted huskily.

The indentation between her feathery brows deepened as she studied his face. 'Well, why on earth did you say it?'

His eyes slid from hers. 'My brother has a reputation with women…'

Jude loosed an incredulous hoot of laughter. 'Whereas you are as pure as the driven snow?'

'We are not discussing me! Marco can be very appealing, but at heart he is an opportunist, and you standing there like that is an opportunity.' He raked a hand through his hair as he looked at her. '*Dio*, what man with blood in his veins would not be tempted?' he grated, closing his hand into a white-knuckled fist.

'And don't I have any say in the matter?' she began to demand, quivering with fury. Tears of humiliation filled her eyes. You could see where he was coming from—all he had to do was look at her to turn her into some sort of panting nymphomaniac, so he probably naturally assumed that she was like that with any-one who deigned to say he wanted her. 'I'll have you know…*oh*!'

The angry colour faded abruptly from her cheeks as his last comments penetrated her bubble of self-righteous indignation. 'You were *jealous*…?' she whispered.

His head turned so that she could see his chiselled golden profile. For a moment she felt he was going to deny it and her stomach muscles tightened in anticipation of the mortifying blow. Then he turned back.

'How could I not be?' His hands curved around her upper arms as he drew her towards him. The pressure of his fingers through the thick towelling just stopped short of painful. 'Italians do not share their women with other men and,' he added with an imperious movement of his dark head, 'I am Italian.'

And this proud heritage he claimed had never been more obvious than it was at that moment, she thought, gazing up at the stark male beauty of his chiselled features. A stab of sexual longing so intense it turned her knees to cotton wool shot through her body.

'And what does that make me?' she asked tensely.

'My woman and my wife…'

Goose-bumps broke out on the surface of her silky soft skin in response to this outrageously arrogant disclosure. Her stomach felt hollow and achy, her tender breasts tingled—this reaction went against everything she believed in.

A woman isn't a possession was an opinion she had voiced on more than one occasion, and she still believed it.

An image of all the 'uncles' she and David had hated over the years swam across her vision and panic gripped her—she was not her mother.

'We're not married yet.'

'Do not provoke me, *cara*…'

The tension drained out of her as their eyes clashed—it wasn't a clash, it was a connection. The exasperated warning carried no sinister overtones; in fact there was an expressive quiver of amusement in his rich, deep voice.

It suddenly hit her she was guilty of stereotyping. Even though Luca was undoubtedly imperious, arrogant and autocratic, he also possessed a dry sense of humour, had a thoughtful side and was incredibly sensitive to her feelings. And when had he ever treated her as less than an equal?

'Why do you bite?' The tear that had been suspended on the tip of a gold-tipped eyelash dislodged itself and began to slide down her cheek.

'You know I do,' he rasped.

The throaty reminder made Jude shiver. Her eyes closed as his dark head blotted out the light. Very slowly he dabbed his tongue to the single errant tear; she gave a fractured sigh.

'I love the taste of you.' He rested his forehead against hers. 'Why are you crying?'

'I'm not now,' she said, turning her cheek into the hand that was cupped her around her face.

'You *were*.'

It was impossible for her to explain the real why, so Jude said the first thing that came into her head. 'You hate my hair.' She sniffed.

She felt rather than heard him laugh at her petulant complaint. 'I don't hate your hair,' he contradicted, picking up a silky strand and letting it run through his fingers. 'I just prefer your curls. I like to bury my face in them.' Her drew her head against his shoulder. Jude's arms snaked around his ribs, and she revelled in the strength of the lean body she was close to.

'How strange you like them, almost as strange as you…' She just managed to bite back *wanting me*. Wanting me in her head could easily have come out sounding like *loving* me…? The last thing she wanted to do was put Luca in a position where he had to spell out what he didn't feel for her. 'Rick wanted me to cut it—he said my face wouldn't look so round and it would help to define my cheekbones.'

'You must never get your hair cut!' he thundered in a voice of outrage. Then— 'Who is *Rick*?'

Under the encouragement of a very firm hand she reluctantly lifted her head from its resting place.

'Rick is the member of the hit squad that my mum sent over to make me a bride fit for you…'

A spasm of astonishment crossed his face. 'You're joking.'

Jude shook her head. 'Her wedding present to me. Crazy, I know,' she admitted, blushing a little under his incredulous stare. 'But you have to remember she doesn't know why you want to marry me.' Jude was actually quite pleased that this explanation emerged without her sounding too obviously embittered. 'But don't worry,' she added as a strange expression flitted across his face. 'I won't tell her.' Solemnly she licked her forefinger and drew a cross over her chest. 'Cross my heart.'

Luca shook his head, his accent more pronounced as he went on to correct her anatomical inaccuracy. 'Your heart is not there, *bella mia*.' He brought her hand up and placed it on the left side of her chest, whether by accident or design directly over her breast. 'It is here.'

For once he was wrong—her heart had vacated her chest and was even now in her throat, restricting her breaths to shallow gasps.

'This is me made over.' Shakily she stepped back from him—never an easy thing to do, she was discovering—and gave a twirl.

For a few seconds Luca silently contemplated her display. 'Your mother is an idiot and so is this *Rick*,' he pronounced with withering contempt. 'You have a perfectly shaped face and your cheekbones require no definition.'

Jude's laugh was half surprise, half amusement. After a moment her gratified smile was replaced by a look of fretful concern. 'You didn't say anything *too* awful to Marco, did you? I'm scared enough about meeting your family as it is; I wouldn't want to lose the one friend there I have.'

He dismissed her concern with a shrug. 'My family need not concern you; they will treat you with the respect my wife deserves.' But what about when you're not around to see? she wondered uneasily. 'I didn't say anything too awful to Marco.'

'Oh, good,' she sighed, relieved.

'I just explained what I would do to him if he ever laid a finger on you,' he continued casually.

'Oh, God!' Jude wailed. 'You didn't. How could you? I'll never be able to look at him again.'

'I wouldn't let that worry you. I'm going to see to it you don't damn well have an opportunity to look at him,' he growled.

'How are you going to do that? Lock me in my room?'

'Marco works for me and I have very wide business interests…'

It took a few seconds for the implications of what he was saying to filter through. Then she recalled Marco mentioning the sudden travelling he had been doing. This was probably going to sound silly, but she had to ask.

'Did you *send* Marco away, because of me?'

Luca didn't seem offended by the question. 'He was already away, I just made sure he didn't come back. Your relationship with him was an unknown factor—it seemed the logical thing to do…'

The most shocking thing, she thought as she searched his face, was the fact nothing in his casual attitude suggested he considered he was saying anything outrageous. A spasm of unease slid through her at this chilling reminder that Luca had been planning everything in calculating detail almost before he'd even met her—in fact she could have been anyone! So long as I fitted the criteria, she concluded dismally.

Perhaps she needed this brutal wake-up, having been in serious danger of forgetting that, no matter how incredible a lover Luca was and how deeply she had fallen for him, this was at the end of the day a marriage of convenience.

'I wanted to marry you and he would have been a distraction. Now of course I know you weren't lovers.' There was a flash of primal male satisfaction in his eyes as they rested hungrily on her drawn face.

'And what if Marco and I had been lovers?' Jude queried, her anger mounting with each fresh casual revelation he made.

Luca didn't even take time to consider her taut question. 'I would have made you forget him.'

'You're totally ruthless, aren't you?' She took an angry step back from him. 'You treat people like puppets you can make dance to your tune! Well, you can't make me do anything I don't want to,' she quivered accusingly.

He studied her angry face for a moment before responding quietly, 'I know that, and I haven't.'

'How can you say that when I'm wearing this thing?' She waved her finger, which suddenly felt weighed down by the enormous ring, in front of him.

'You came to my bed because *you* wanted to. You are marrying me because *you* want to.' He saw Jude flinch and he smiled grimly. 'You cannot turn around and look at me as though I am some sort of Machiavellian monster who has compelled you to do these things against your will.'

He was right, of course he was, she thought, biting down hard on her lower lip. He had been persistent, but hadn't misled her or applied pressure. He hadn't needed to! Pretending he'd forced or tricked the ring onto her finger was easier than tackling the reason she'd accepted it. The compulsive need that she felt every time she looked at him.

'It is not my methods you object to,' he suggested in a harsh tone. 'It is my honesty. Now let me continue to be honest. If you wish you can turn your head away like a child,' he conceded. Jude flushed and turned back. 'But you *shall* listen to what I say. Though,' he added in a wry digression, 'whether you are in a mood to hear it is another matter. And *please* do not look at me as though you have been summoned to the overbearing headmaster's office!'

This last exasperated petition made her blink. 'You don't have to say anything else,' she told him with a resigned shrug. 'You're right, Luca. I…overreacted.'

Her unexpected capitulation caused the muscles in his lean dark face to tense with shock.

'So did I,' he responded after a moment's startled silence. 'With Marco. Marco has a history of trying to poach my women.'

She nodded. 'Which is why you were so mad with him.' That figured.

'And I have either ignored it,' he proceeded to elaborate, 'and let him get on with it, or told him to stop it, which he

does. I have never felt the urge to rip him limb from limb before,' he revealed in a conversational tone.

Jude's eyes went round. *'Oh!'*

'I rather think my reaction to seeing him with you might
have…'

'Scared the wits out of him?'

His lashes lowered over an amused gleam at her wry
interjection.

'The idea of him or any man touching you does not make
me think rationally…' He cleared his throat and added thickly,
'You are a passionate woman…' he began, his jet eyes brushing her face.

'Only with you,' an enchanted Jude replied without thinking.

He froze. And then slowly, like a complacent cat approaching its cornered prey, he relaxed. 'Is that so, *cara*?'

'What I was trying to say is I'm not attracted to Marco.
And I'm not stupid, I know he is a charming love rat…' It
was very hard to form a sentence, let alone string them together, when you were the focus of that unique lazy-eyed,
gleaming scrutiny.

'I prefer the way you said it the first time,' Luca admitted,
reaching for her.

With a sigh Jude walked into his arms and they closed tight
around her. She felt his kisses in her hair, on her neck, moving along her collar-bone before finally finding her mouth.

The kiss sent her senses reeling into outer space. 'Make
love to me.' Then, conscious her request had come out sounding like a command, she added on an apologetic note, 'If you
have the time?'

'I think I might just fit it into my busy schedule,' he returned, straight-faced.

'Are you laughing at me?' she demanded, scanning his
face suspiciously.

'It is fast becoming one of the great joys of my life,' he confirmed, taking her hand firmly within his.

She was still puzzling this enigmatic observation when he added, with one of his slow, sizzling smiles, 'Now let's go and enjoy the other one.'

CHAPTER TEN

JUDE'S concerns about flying with small children turned out to be unfounded. The only time they became restive was whilst they were waiting in the VIP lounge after Luca's private jet missed its original slot because she had insisted on going back to the flat because she couldn't remember if she had switched off her iron.

It was a subject she still felt pretty defensive about.

'We should be there by three.' Luca, who had been speaking to the pilot, said as he rejoined her.

'I suppose you're never going to let me forget it was my fault we're late,' she observed crankily.

'So far I haven't mentioned it once...' There was sardonic amusement in the dark eyes that drifted across her tense face. '*Your* last count was five.'

Jude frowned. 'Well, you were *thinking* it, I know you were. Maybe the iron wasn't on, but it *could* have been.'

'So you said at the time.' He reached across and pushed a curl from her cheek.

Jude despaired that even this casual contact had the power to make her stomach muscles clench.

'When we are an old married couple,' he confided in a soft

voice, 'maybe then you will possess insight into my thoughts, but at this moment you are way out, *cara. Way out!*'

Something in his eyes made her decide it might not be such a good idea to ask him what he was thinking.

'Coward,' he whispered in her ear as she picked up a glossy magazine thoughtfully provided by the eager-to-please cabin crew.

It seemed that Luca wasn't hampered by an inability to read *her* mind. Jude concentrated on the glossy photo spread and pretended not to hear the taunt until she realised she was looking at the latest society wedding when, with a sick feeling in the pit of her stomach, she slammed it down hastily. She looked up and found Luca's eyes were upon her. She looked away quickly, excruciatingly aware that the briefest contact could make her say stupid things. She was thinking along the lines of take me!

'It was the usual boring thing, celebrities in posh frocks,' she observed with a dismissive nod towards the discarded journal. 'God, what a way to live…' Her smooth brow puckered as she contemplated the apparent lifestyle of the people pictured in the pages. 'Living from one photo opportunity to the next. Never leaving the house without full make-up just in case someone takes a photo of you with your mouth open and sells it to a tabloid.'

She gave an expressive little shudder, which morphed into a look of wide-eyed anxiety as she realised she was talking to a man who had appeared in more than one glossy spread and was constantly stalked by the paparazzi.

'God, I didn't mean you!'

'My relief is boundless that I am exempt from your scorn.'

The sardonic amusement on his face made her facial muscles tighten as annoyance warmed her skin to a delicate soft pink. 'Silly me, I forgot I was talking to the man who doesn't require anyone's approval.'

'Except a judge who could decide Valentina would be better off with someone else.' His sombre, brooding gaze rested on his daughter, who was at that moment threading ribbons in Sophia's soft curls, a frown of charming concentration on her grave little face.

Jude's soft heart felt as though it were in a vice as she watched him. The tidal wave of love that swept over her was so intense that if she hadn't already been sitting it would have washed her away quite literally. Growing inside was a fierce determination that the thing Luca secretly feared would never actually come to pass. Impulsively she reached out and took the brown hand that rested lightly on his knee between her two hands.

'We won't let anyone do that, Luca,' she promised earnestly.

Luca turned his eyes, brushing first her small hands holding his before lifting to her face. It was only when he studied her face with a strange expression that Jude became aware that she had tight hold of his hand. Abruptly she released his warm hand, with an awkward little laugh.

'Sorry.'

'You've never apologised for touching me before.'

For a split second the image that flashed before her eyes— an erotic image of his golden body gleaming with sweat and need as she ran a finger lightly down his belly—blitzed every other thought from her head. She was shaking slightly as she refocused on his face.

Fighting to regain her composure, Jude resisted the temptation to draw attention to her hot cheeks by placing a cooling hand on them. She shrugged casually in an attempt to emulate his pragmatic attitude.

'Well, obviously that's not the same thing.' She hoped her response was sufficient to reassure him she wasn't going to overstep the unseen boundaries he'd erected and expect what they had in the bedroom to overflow into other parts of their lives.

He wanted sex, and he wanted shallow, so that was what she would give him! *And what makes you think you can do shallow with a man you are madly in love with when you couldn't do it with the ones that meant nothing to you?*

'You mean it's not sex.' The pounding in his skull got louder when she smiled and looked relieved. *Relieved!*

'*Exactly.*'

She felt slightly uncertain when the flat, stony expression on Luca's face didn't alter.

'Maybe we should attempt to introduce such spontaneous gestures. They do lend authenticity to the image we wish to present.'

By not as much as a flicker of an eyelash did she reveal how much his comments hurt her. 'That's a good point,' she agreed cheerily. She knew that it was totally irrational under the circumstances to expect him to think of it any other way, but that didn't stop her wishing.

God, Jude, you can't start living in a fantasy world. He doesn't love you, he just fancies you, so live with it! she advised herself brutally.

'It was a silly idea *you* needing *my* help, I'm sure you've covered every angle.'

'You'd think so, wouldn't you?'

Whilst she couldn't quite pin down the elusive emotion that flickered across his face, she had the strongest feeling that it was somehow significant. As the moment stretched his unblinking scrutiny started to affect her control. For one crazy moment she even considered challenging him with her true feelings, then sanity intervened.

'You know, I've never been on a flight where there are more crew than passengers,' she told him brightly.

'Is that so?'

Despite his dauntingly uninterested manner Jude found she just couldn't stop talking; the words bubbled out of her.

'It all seems a bit decadent, though I've got to admit it's something I could get used to, especially when travelling with small children.' Pleased to have a legitimate excuse to break eye contact, she glanced towards the older children, who were playing a board game with the minder. 'Carlo really is very good with them, but it's a lot more work with four of them. You can't expect him to take responsibility for all of them.'

Luca forced the tension from his muscles by sheer force of will. 'You think I'm taking advantage of him?' he suggested, linking his hands behind his head as he leaned back in his seat.

Nothing in the relaxed action suggested that at that moment he was planning the precise means he would use to illustrate to his bride, in a manner that not even *she* could misinterpret, that he wasn't going to be rationed as to when and where he could touch her! *To even suggest such a thing...*

Jude could no more *not* look at what his action displayed than she could not breathe; the draw of his lithe body was simply irresistible. Sometimes the violence of her emotions when he was around scared her—no, cancel sometimes, *always* was closer to the grim reality.

In future, she decided, there would be no more indiscreet disclosures concerning his sublime excellence as a lover! And the subject of her own blissful satisfaction with his efforts to please her would remain a taboo subject. If she carried on this way it was only a matter of time before she said something that couldn't be attributed to the heat of passion.

Despite this resolution, her eyes slid down his long, lean length terminating the covetous exploration at his shoes with an almost imperceptible sigh. It was just as well that leg room was not an issue here because Luca was not a man built for cramped spaces.

'Of course not,' she managed once she'd dragged her eyes back to his face. 'I just think you might not have considered the additional workload of three more children.'

'I have, which is why I have arranged for a nursemaid to be added to our staff.'

Our staff? Oh, God, do I know what the hell I'm getting myself into?

'I don't have any staff and I don't want any.'

'I thought the principal selling factor of this marriage, from your point of view,' he inserted drily, 'was to provide you with the means to continue with your career uninterrupted whilst the children were well taken care of.'

She waited for inspiration but it didn't arrive 'That was before,' she blurted, feeling pushed into a corner by his relentless logic.

A wolfish grin split his lean countenance. 'Before you started appreciating the other benefits of marriage to me?'

Jude flushed to the roots of her hair at the sly suggestion. 'You're so conceited,' she choked.

'A lot more so with being told how marvellous, extraordinary and the *best* I am on a regular basis,' he inserted innocently.

A hissing sound of exasperation escaped through her clenched teeth. 'You *are* incredible in bed; it's just out of it you drive me insane!'

His negligent attitude suddenly vanished as his dark eyes overflowed with amusement. His rich, warm laughter filled the enclosed space.

Jude closed her eyes and released her suspended breath. When she opened them the teasing quality had gone from his face.

'You've got to be realistic about this child-care situation, Jude.'

'I know I do…I just want the children to know who their…'

She drew a hand over the V of skin exposed at the base of her throat—she wasn't their mother. Even as she spoke—or tried to—she could feel the ugly blotches breaking out all over her neck. Which was hardly surprising, considering she was being pressurised to explain something she hadn't quite figured out herself yet.

'I want them to think of me as the person they come to when they need help. *Me*,' she emphasised, placing her hand flat on her breast. 'Not a nursemaid or nanny.'

'Can it be you have found parenting more rewarding than you imagined?' Luca, content to see the flicker of awareness chase across her features, did not actively pursue the subject. 'Accepting help with the children does not equate with renouncing your role. When we have children—'

Jude froze. 'Children?' she echoed in a strangled voice. She gulped. *'Us?'* she added in a barely audible whisper.

'You must have thought about the possibility, considering it is not something we've been actively avoiding.' One mobile brow lifted as all the colour drained from her face, leaving it milk-white. 'I'm assuming you are not on the contraceptive pill?'

She shook her head numbly.

'I thought not.'

Her thoughts were in total chaos. How could I *not* have thought…? God, I could be right now! Her eyes fell from his, drawn to the flat section of her midriff. There was something frighteningly seductive in the thought of Luca's baby growing inside her. This sudden revelation was just too much for her to assimilate; she held up her hand as if that could halt the chain that had been set in motion.

'Why didn't you…?' She faltered. Why didn't he? Why didn't *I*? A fractured sigh erupted from her throat as she squared her shoulders. She wasn't the type of person who passed the buck. 'No, it's not your fault.'

'Does it have to be anyone's fault?' he wondered.

Jude blinked. 'Pardon?'

'Would it be so terrible if you had a baby?'

The protective numbness washed over her afresh. '*Your* baby?' she heard herself whimper stupidly.

The lashes that any woman would have died for lowered, making it impossible for her to read his expression as he mildly observed, 'Well, if it were anyone else's baby I might be...*upset*.'

'Well, that's hardly likely, is it?' As if she were going to go from Luca into any other man's arms. With a sigh she pushed a shaky hand through the curls she had deliberately not tamed after Luca's comments on the subject. Is there *anything* you wouldn't do to make him happy? the irritated voice of her independence demanded.

But would having his baby be something that required a compromise?

Oh, my God!

'Babies?'

'Well, one would be fine to begin with.'

His flippancy caught her on the raw. Teeth gritted, she caught hold of his arm. 'This isn't a joke. I know you've already got a child but it's not something I... This is all new...'

Something moved at the back of his eyes that she couldn't define. 'A baby is never a joke, *cara*. It's a serious undertaking, the consequences of which last a lifetime.'

Her eyes widened to their fullest extent as his words introduced a horrifying possibility. 'You didn't *not* take precautions because you needed an ace up your sleeve if I decided to back out?'

This was one of those occasions when the moment the words were out you wished them unsaid. The expression of austere revulsion that contorted his chiselled features was proof enough that her instincts were correct—bad thing to say, Jude.

'Actually, I have never in my *life* been heedless and reckless enough to have unprotected sex with any woman, but you. So,' he added, making a sharp, stabbing gesture with his arm, 'I suggest you make of that what you will.'

'There's a little girl sitting over there who says otherwise,' Jude replied in a subdued, unhappy whisper.

A frustrated hissing sound issued from his compressed lips. 'Think what you will, but I meant what I said.' Rising in one elegant, fluid motion that made her sensitive tummy muscles flip, he moved across the cabin to the children.

Jude, following his advice, could only assume he meant that whereas Valentina was a child whose arrival had been planned, theirs—if there was one?—would be the result of a moment of reckless passion.

She spent the rest of the flight pretending she was asleep.

Carlo began to get into one of the limousines that had just brought the wedding party from the airport to the palazzo. Luca left Jude's side and placed a hand on the older man's shoulder.

A rather intense conversation then took place between the two men. Jude, watching the interchange from a distance, became increasingly curious as there was much arm-waving from the normally phlegmatic Carlo as they spoke at length. She scooped up Amy, who had fallen onto the gravel in front of the ancient building Luca had identified as the palazzo.

'Is something wrong?' she asked in a low undertone as Luca came back to her side.

'Carlo has not been inside these walls for many years.' And then to Jude's intense frustration he didn't elaborate on this intriguing statement. She didn't have long to wait to see the reason for Carlo's reluctance.

'Our reception committee?' she asked when an elegant figure appeared flanked by a man and a woman both in uniform.

'My stepmother, Lucilla,' he explained in an expressionless voice.

'A fake,' her own mother whispered in her ear. 'The pearls are real, the smile isn't.'

Lucilla Di Rossi's condescending gaze swept over the visitors, halting dramatically when she reached the burly minder. Her loss of stately cool was quite dramatic.

'You cannot imagine that your father would allow you to bring this…*person* into the house!'

'Take the children up to the nursery, will you, Carlo? They are tired.' Carlo, his face impassive, followed the suggestion, leaving only Amy in Jude's arms.

You didn't have to understand Italian to figure out the gist of the words Luca's stepmother proceeded to spit at him were something akin to over her dead body.

Jude didn't have the faintest idea how Luca maintained his slightly bored attitude throughout the prolonged harangue. 'Carlo stays.'

This uncompromising response clearly infuriated the elegant figure who, with one poisonous look at her stepson, turned her attention to Jude.

'I suppose he has told you that creature you have left your children with has a criminal record?'

'*Mother!*' Marco, who had appeared in the doorway just in time to hear his mother's dramatic revelation, groaned in dismay.

Ignoring her son's warning, the older woman widened her thin lips in a vulpine smile as she observed Jude's shocked response. 'I see he didn't.' She shot a triumphant look at Luca, whose attention was fixed on Jude's taut profile.

'I'll go after them,' Jude heard her mother say as she started past.

Without taking her eyes off the figure in the doorway Jude caught hold of her mother's arm. 'That's not necessary, Mum. Carlo is quite capable of coping.'

'Shall I tell you what he did?'

'No!' Jude smiled and moderated her forceful tone. Her chin lifted. 'If Luca trusts Carlo then I don't need to know anything else,' she said quietly.

'Jude, darling, are you sure?' her mother's fretful voice hissed.

Jude's frantic heartbeat slowed as she took a deep breath. 'I'm totally sure, Mum.' And she was. Her eyes flickered towards the tall, silent figure standing a little apart.

Their eyes touched. Jude, mesmerised by the message in his stunning eyes, barely registered that for once Luca actually looked less than his usual urbane, controlled self.

The moment passed and Luca was making the formal introductions and, like everyone else, she was acting as though the nasty scene had not occurred.

Whilst on the outside she was smiling and making the right noises, inside she was in a state of total confusion. Could what she was thinking be true? Did he care? Was she a fool to read so much into one look and a silence?

'She's heavy—shall I take her?'

Jude started and realised that Luca was talking to her. Feeling ridiculously shy, she nodded and placed the toddler in his outstretched arms. Their hands accidentally touched and for a moment they neither of them moved, they just stood there, their fingers brushing softly. The moment was broken when the little girl curled her arms about Luca's neck and placed a loud kiss on his lean cheek as they mounted the wide, curving staircase.

'Where's Mum?' Jude asked, looking around and finding all the other members of their party had disappeared without her even noticing!

'They've put her in the east wing. I can have her moved closer to you, if you wish?'

'No, I'll be fine.'

'It'll only be for the one night; tomorrow we will spend the night in the tower room.'

If she thought that far ahead she might well freak out on the spot. 'Can you see the Grand Canal from there?' The sardonic look he slanted her made Jude frown defensively. 'Well, you might take all this for granted, but I've never been to Venice before and it seems a shame not to see a few things whilst I'm here. Think of me as a tourist.'

This cheery suggestion drew a choking sound from his throat. 'I believe you can see the Grand Canal, but actually I hadn't planned on spending much time admiring the view.'

Jude took one look into the challenge shimmering in his silver-flecked eyes and took the next two steps together. Then stopped dead.

'My mother,' Luca explained, seeing her staring at the portrait of a luminously beautiful woman that overlooked the hallway.

'She was very beautiful, and you look very like her,' Jude concluded, comparing the eyes and the full lips on the woman in the portrait with the man beside her.

'I'm beautiful?' he teased.

Jude didn't smile. 'I've always thought so.'

Though she made a point of not looking to see how he reacted to this revelation, she did hear his sharp inhalation. This time she took the lead in their slow progress.

It wasn't until they reached the top that Luca spoke. 'About Carlo…'

'It doesn't matter.'

'It does,' he countered flatly. 'When I was in my teens Carlo was my father's driver. He befriended me; his friendship made life more…bearable,' he revealed quietly. 'My stepmother didn't like the fact he was kind to me, and even defended me upon occasion. Some items went missing…'

Sensing what was coming, Jude shook her head.

The eyes he turned to her held the smouldering remains of a deep sense of anger and injustice that she suspected would stay with him for ever.

'They were found in his room,' he confirmed. 'She as good as admitted she planted them there when I accused her, but I was a boy and my voice was not heard. Carlo was given a suspended sentence, but a record doesn't make it easy to get a job.'

'Couldn't your father…?'

'I think he knew what she had done, but my father does not concern himself with anything much but his books.'

'Including you? Don't shrug as if it's trivial!' she cried. 'It isn't! I think—'

'Jude—'

'No, let me say this, Luca. I know he's your father, and I don't care how heartbroken he was when your mother died. What sort of a man isn't there when his son needs him?' she demanded on a quivering note of outrage.

'A father who doesn't perhaps deserve that son?'

This harsh explanation originated from just behind her. Jude spun around as if shot. A little under six feet, with dark hair heavily streaked with grey and a thin face that was deeply etched with lines, the man standing there had the saddest eyes she had ever seen.

Luca's explanatory, 'This is my father. Father, this is my future wife, Dr Jude Lucas,' was kind of redundant.

The dark eyes surveyed her flushed face silently for a moment. 'Not at all what I was expecting, Luca,' he observed cryptically before nodding to his son and moving away.

'Why does this sort of thing always happen to me?'

Luca didn't vouchsafe an answer to her anguished question; instead he put forth one of his own. 'Do you intend to fight my battles often?'

'I'm s…sorry,' she stammered apologetically. 'I know it's none of my business, but when I thought of you…' Her throat closed over emotionally.

'So I'm the object of your pity.'

Jude's teeth grated in exasperation as she held out her hands for Amy. 'Come to Aunty Jude, darling,' she coaxed. Over the toddler's head she added, 'How do you manage to twist everything I say?'

A look of total astonishment appeared on his face. '*Me* twist what *you* say…?' he began when a uniformed figure appeared at his side and apologetically informed him the call he had been expecting had arrived.

Luca nodded. 'Could you show Dr Lucas to the nursery and then to her bedroom?' His eyes touched Jude's face as he handed over Amy and he nodded again.

Watching him go, Jude felt as if her only friend in the place had gone, friend in this instance being a relative term.

'Luca!' she called suddenly.

He turned at the sound of her voice.

'Will I…will you be there later…at dinner?'

Even before the forlorn question reached him Luca was striding towards her. He took her face between his hands and kissed her until the world was spinning.

'I'll *always* be there for you.'

CHAPTER ELEVEN

'CAREFUL of your hair!' Lyn remonstrated as her daughter slipped the champagne silk satin gown over her head.

'I haven't put the flowers in yet.' Jude held her breath as the slim garment slid over the curls that had been loosely confined on the top of her head. 'And I am being careful,' she promised as the rich, heavy fabric pooled around her feet. 'How do I look?' She craned her neck to see her rear view in the mirror as she struggled to reach the zip.

'For heaven's sake!' her mother protested watching her daughter's efforts with an expression of exasperation. 'If you're going to marry the man who's going to inherit all this—' her gesture took in the incredibly grand surroundings '—you're going to have to cultivate a more regal manner.'

'It's pretty imposing, isn't it?' Jude sighed. Walking through the echoing stone corridors, she had felt the oppressive weight of the generations of Di Rossis, many of whom stared at her from the walls bearing down upon her. Knowing of Luca's background and actually seeing it were different matters entirely.

'The plumbing leaves much to be desired.'

This practical observation made Jude laugh. 'That's better,' Lyn approved. 'Now, stop fidgeting whilst I get this zip.

You really don't want to let his family intimidate you—from what I hear, if it wasn't for Luca the whole place would have fallen back into the canal by now. Apparently half those priceless works of art on the walls had been sold off,' she revealed in a confidential manner as she struggled with the long zip.

'I dread to think how much it cost him to buy them back. Mind you, he can afford it,' she concluded with a touch of complacency.

'I don't think his father likes me,' Jude, who hadn't told anyone about her accidental meeting with Stefano Di Rossi, commented.

'I really don't see how you could tell, darling. I didn't see his expression change once at dinner. And I doubt if he said more than two words all through the meal. Perhaps he was disappointed that Luca wasn't there?' she suggested.

Jude focused on her toes. 'Perhaps.' It was ironic really that she'd read so much into Luca's 'I'll *always* be there for you' when he'd actually not even managed to be there for her at that interminable family dinner!

'Breathe in a bit…that's it. Did you notice when we were taking breakfast that the room was full of photos of Marco, but there wasn't a single one of Luca?'

'I didn't go down to breakfast, Mum.'

'No, but you really should have—we don't want you fainting.'

'I won't do that.'

'You know, the first thing I'd do if I was married to the very sexy Stefano would be to take down that dirty great portrait of my predecessor. My God, but Luca is the living image of the woman, isn't he?'

'Stefano is married, Mum.'

'Good God, child, I'm not *interested*. He may be attractive, but he's far too cerebral for my taste. I prefer my men to be a bit more physical; of course *both* is nice but we can't all be as lucky as you.'

Jude, who was becoming increasingly uncomfortable with this frank exchange, sighed with relief when Lyn cried, 'That's it,' as the zip shot safely home. 'You look very beautiful,' she added huskily when Jude turned around.

'Really?'

'Look for yourself.'

Jude was amazed to see the tears standing out in her mother's eyes. 'You can't cry—you'll ruin your makeup, Mum.'

'Good point,' sniffed her mother with a watery grin as she dabbed a tissue to her eyes. 'I'll see you there, then.'

'You're leaving?' Jude felt a flare of panic.

'Don't worry, you won't be alone,' Lyn said, casting a last emotional look at her daughter. 'He's on time!' she exclaimed when there was a loud knock on the door.

'Who…?' Jude began as her mother opened the door with a flourish. From where she was standing she couldn't see who it was, just the shocked expression on her mum's face. Clearly this was not the person she had been expecting.

'Well, of course…I was just going,' Jude heard her say in a flustered manner before she blew her daughter a kiss and stepped out of the room.

'Signor Di Rossi!' she exclaimed as the distinguished figure entered the room fully. She didn't have the faintest idea why Luca's austere father should be paying her a visit. The only half-possible explanation she could come up with was this was some sort of last-ditch effort to prevent the marriage…a personal plea to beg her not to sully the blood line. Or maybe he was going to try and buy her off?

'Jude—I may call you Jude?'

'Of course,' she agreed warily.

'You look extremely beautiful.'

'Thank you.'

'You are wondering why I am here? Of course you are. I just wished…I hope that you will accept this from me.' He held a velvet box out to her. When she didn't make a move to take it he nodded. 'Please?'

With unsteady hands Jude did as he wanted. Inside the box was a heavy gold ring; it was intricately carved and looked extremely old.

'It's beautiful,' she said, flicking him a questioning look.

'My wife, Luca's mother, gave it to me on our wedding day. I thought perhaps you would like to give it to Luca? I have given him his mother's wedding band to give to you.'

The gesture was so unexpected her eyes filled with tears. 'Thank you, I would like that very much,' she said quietly. The significance of this gesture was not wasted on her.

He only said, 'Good,' but Jude had the impression he was pleased. Hand on the door handle, he turned back. 'I can see why my son has fallen in love with you.'

Only he hasn't!

The irony reduced Jude to tears, which she desperately fought to hold back. When a short time later there was a second knock on the door she took several moments to compose herself before answering.

'The flowers, how lovely,' she began when she saw the figure carrying her bouquet. Then she stopped, the blood draining from her face. 'Dad?' she whispered incredulously. 'You're here?'

'Just stepped off the plane—literally,' the tanned figure who looked very like her brother explained.

'But how?'

'Your husband is a very forceful bloke when he puts his mind to something.'

'Luca did this?' she breathed, her thoughts racing.

'He seemed to think you might like to have your old dad at your wedding?'

For the first time Jude recognised the diffidence in her father's manner for what it was—he wasn't sure of his reception. 'Luca thought right!' she cried, throwing her arms around him.

'Watch the flowers, girl, you'll crush them,' her father remonstrated huskily as he pushed her a little away. 'My,' he said, a catch in his voice. 'I'd fly around the world twice over to see you looking like that.'

Jude shook her head. 'I still can't believe you're here.'

'It's been too long, but maybe it's not too late for us to get reacquainted?'

'I'd like that.'

'But not now, I think you've got a previous appointment.'

Jude took a deep breath, accepted the bouquet of gypsophila and white baby roses and laid her hand in the crook of the arm he presented her.

'Ready?'

Jude lifted her chin. 'Ready.' She just hoped that when the time came she would be able to deliver her vows in an equally confident fashion, that she wouldn't stumble or stutter.

Her worries proved unfounded. The ceremony went without a hitch. The tiny chapel was filled with the aroma of flowers and incense. Through the sea of faces Jude saw only one. The entire service had a dreamlike quality; it was only when it was over and she and Luca were making their way to the salon overlooking the Grand Canal where the wedding breakfast was to take place that it hit her.

'You're shaking.' Luca, a groove of anxiety between his dark brows, examined her face, which was a shade paler than her dress. 'Do you want to sit down?'

'I could do with some fresh air.'

Nodding, he led her outside into a small private courtyard.

Flowers spilled from pots on the tiny wrought balconies of the rooms above and water from a tiny fountain tinkled softly. Luca pushed her down onto a wrought-iron bench.

A few deep breaths later she lifted her head.

'Feeling better?'

She blinked. 'I did it…I went through with it. Sorry, you know that—you were there.' She gave a shaky laugh.

'It's customary to wait until after you've cut the cake to start having regrets.'

Jude's eyes widened. 'I don't have regrets.' Then, regretting the vehemence of her rebuttal, added quickly, 'Why—do you?' Belatedly she registered his uncharacteristically strained air and added, rising jerkily to her feet, 'Well, *do you*?'

'The only thing I regret is that we have to go back in there. This party is going to go on for ever and the only person I want to share today with is you.'

The way he was looking at her made her heart thud faster. 'Well, you invited them…talking of which, bringing my father, it was a lovely thing to do, Luca, thank you,' she said huskily.

'I hoped it would please you.' Suddenly he took her hands in his and drew her towards him. 'I want to say a lot of things to you, but if I start to someone will inevitably come and interrupt—the things I wish to say should not be interrupted.' Frustration filled his lean face as he looked hungrily down into her upturned features. 'Meet me here later tonight at… eleven…?'

Mutely Jude nodded.

She told herself there was absolutely no point speculating about what he intended to tell her, but of course she did. Whilst she smiled, laughed and danced and acted like a carefree bride she thought about little else. Frequently when her eyes drifted towards Luca's tall, dynamic figure—they did this fairly often—she found that he was watching her.

On each occasion the effect of the contact on her nervous system was dramatic and sometimes embarrassing. She dropped two glasses and trod on a diplomat's toes.

Late in the evening she found herself dancing with Marco, who was a very accomplished dancer.

'Don't worry, I asked Luca's permission.'

Jude couldn't decide if he was joking or not. 'That woman over there, the one in purple.' Marco's glance followed the direction she tilted her head. He looked away quickly, his colour slightly heightened. 'Who is she? She's been watching me all night.'

'That's Natalia Corradi, Valentina's grandmother and a stiff-necked old battleaxe. The guy sitting next to her is her son, Laurent, the blonde is his wife.'

Jude nodded. That at least explained the unfriendly vibes she'd been picking up.

'Listen, Marco, if you could dance me towards that door, I'm just going to slip away to say goodnight to the children.'

'Sure thing,' he agreed, whirling her lightly around.

She spent half an hour with the children, promised Valentina and Sophia they could press the flowers in their posies and keep them for ever, agreed that Joseph would never have to wear a page's outfit again and found the corner where Amy's favourite teddy had fallen.

By the time she slipped out of the building there was still a margin of carmine along the horizon, though the first stars were beginning to pierce the velvety night sky. Jude shivered and drew the cobwebby lace wrap up over her bare shoulders as she picked her way across the damp grass to the fountain.

The day had been magic and the night promised to be even more so. Luca's words kept going around in her head. Could she have read more into them than was actually there…?

Lifting her skirts to protect the fabric from the slightly longer grass, she reached the steps that led up to the secret courtyard. At the top she stopped, the breath nagged in her throat; it was a magical scene. The cobbled courtyard and the balcony of the ancient stone building behind it were artistically back-lit by strategically placed spotlights.

As she walked forward the tapping of her heels on the cobbles was mingled with the trickling sound of water as it splashed onto the ancient stone. The air she breathed was filled with the scent of night-scented stocks and jasmine. As her long gown brushed the floor she felt as though she'd stepped into the pages of a fairy-tale book, but then the entire day had had an air of unreality about it.

She drew the wrap a little tighter as a soft gust of wind stirred the leaves of the trees above her head. Suddenly several spotlights that had been inactive flickered into life. It took her eyes a couple of seconds to adjust to the extra illumination.

When she did she saw the detail these lights had been positioned to softly highlight. Her enchanted gaze took in the small table and two chairs set discreetly in one corner. She walked towards them, a soft smile curving her lips. When she reached the table she picked the bottle of champagne set on the mosaic surface from the ice bucket it nestled in and pretended to study the label before returning it.

She flicked one champagne flute with the tip of one pearly fingernail and a bell-like tone rang out across the courtyard.

'Well, are you going to come out or should I drink this alone?' she called out teasingly to the darkness.

Even though she had been expecting to see him, a frisson of shock ran through her body when a tall figure separated out from the shadows.

'You knew I was here?' His face was in shadow so she couldn't see his expression.

'I always know when you're there,' she explained simply.

He drew a harsh breath and as he stepped into the light he looked into her soft glowing eyes. 'You look very beautiful tonight, *cara mia*.'

'I feel beautiful,' she admitted.

'Perhaps you are learning to see yourself through my eyes,' he suggested, taking her arm and drawing her back to the table.

Jude liked the feel of his heavy arm across her shoulders. Instead of backing away from the raw, intoxicating masculinity he exuded, she embraced it.

'Champagne?' he asked, lifting the bottle from its cradle.

'I already feel a little drunk,' she confided.

'You haven't had anything to drink. I know—I have been watching you.'

'What—all the time?'

'Every second,' he confirmed throatily.

'I'm not drunk on wine, just the air, the magical air. This has been a marvellous day, Luca. I keep pinching myself to check I'm not dreaming,' she confided.

He came towards her and pressed the glass full of sparkling liquid in her hand. Standing so close their thighs almost touched, he raised his own glass. 'To much more pleasurable ways of convincing you you're not dreaming,' he proposed, brushing a soft curl from her brow. 'Are you cold?' he added solicitously as a shiver ran through her body.

'No, just excited,' she admitted, swaying gently towards him.

'Now isn't this romantic?'

The slurred voice made Jude start. She would have pulled back from Luca if the hand firmly placed in the curve at the base of her spine had not prevented her. After a moment she relaxed and leaned into his hard, lean body.

'Is this a private party?'

As the older woman tottered towards them on shaky legs it was evident she had been taking advantage of the lavish bar facilities.

As she got closer Jude was shocked by the appearance of the sophisticated woman Marco had identified for her earlier that evening. Natalia Corradi's smooth chignon had become unanchored, leaving her silver-grey hair to fall in wild disarray around her face. Her once perfect make-up was smudged and smeared. The fresh application of scarlet lipstick had obviously been applied with an unsteady hand.

Jude experienced a wave of compassion for the woman, her own happiness contrasted so dramatically with this woman's dejection. This must have been an incredibly hard day for her, to see another woman take her daughter's place, and no matter what her argument with Luca was she must love her grandchild, she thought.

How much better it would be for everyone if they could put their differences behind them. Her eyes narrowed thoughtfully; there was the possibility that coming fresh into the situation she could act as some sort of mediator. Surely there was a middle ground that both parties could live with for Valentina's sake. Luca was an intelligent man—he would see that, surely.

'Why don't you have a seat?' Jude suggested, slipping away from Luca's side and drawing one of the wrought-iron chairs from beside the table.

'Ah, the little wife.' The depth of malice in the harsh voice was reflected in the feverish glittering eyes that hazily focused upon Jude.

'Nobody wants to keep you from your granddaughter. You can see Valentina any time you want, can't she, Luca?' Jude appealed to her husband.

'No, she has abused that privilege.' Luca stepped forward,

interposing his body between the older woman and Jude as though to protect her.

Jude was far more dismayed by the total inflexibility in her husband's hard voice and the grim remoteness of his expression than she was by any threat offered by the pathetic, rather sad-looking female he was shielding her from. How could he be so unfeeling?

'But, Luca, wouldn't it be better to…?'

Luca's cold eyes flicked across her face. *As if I'm a stranger*—the thought slid into her head. 'You have not the faintest idea what you are talking about, Jude, so leave it alone.' His attitude was blightingly dismissive. 'Natalia,' he said, inclining his head fractionally.

'Only two glasses…what a shame.'

'I think perhaps you have had enough,' Luca observed in a voice of deadly calm.

'Well, how else was I meant to get through this day?' she hissed. 'Is she in on your plan?' Her bleary-eyed attention switched to the slender figure clad in cream silk standing just behind him. What she saw made her shake her head. 'No, she's too stupid. I suppose the little fool thinks you married her for love.' High tinkling laughter rang out. 'She's obviously besotted with you; it's written all over her,' she sneered. 'Is that a blush? How quaint,' she trilled.

The sound that issued through his clenched teeth drew Jude's attention to Luca's arrogant chiselled profile. She saw his jaw clench just before he responded in his native tongue. Despite the obvious strength of his emotions he expressed himself in an even, carefully measured manner, which, despite his soft voice and the fact she hadn't the faintest idea what he was saying, chilled Jude to the bone.

She saw that the older woman looked pretty shaken by what he had said too. That Luca could employ such brutal tactics to browbeat a woman who was obviously emotionally fragile shocked and disgusted Jude, whose soft heart went out to the distressed grandmother. Hand extended in an instinctively comforting gesture, Jude stepped forward, ignoring Luca's harsh warning growl.

Just as she was about to lay her hand on the hunched shoulder of the grey-haired figure the other woman's head came up. There was such malice in the eyes that raked her face that Jude stepped backwards, almost colliding with Luca. His arms went around her, drawing her to him. She sank into him, drawing strength and comfort from the contact.

'He thinks he can silence me.' The thin lips compressed in a mean smile. 'Well, not this time. I want justice for my baby. I'm going to tell your precious bride what sort of man she has married and none of your threats will stop me. The world should know what sort of man he is. It's only for my granddaughter's sake that I have kept silent up until now.'

Luca spun Jude around. For a moment he looked down into her pale, confused face as if he was committing what he saw to memory. 'She is poison, Jude.'

'Perhaps you should get her son to help. I'll stay with her.'

Luca shook her gently as her attention drifted back towards the other woman. 'You must not listen to what she says.'

'It doesn't matter what she says, I can see she's upset.'

'Has he told you about Maria…my baby girl?'

Jude pushed away Luca's restraining hand. 'Luca told me that she suffered bad post-natal depression.'

'And that's why she killed herself, is that what he told you? Oh, the doctors said that too, but he paid them to say it!' she accused, stabbing a shaking finger towards the tall, silent man who appeared to have distanced himself from the entire hostility. His air of icy detachment seemed to inflame his adversary.

'It was tragic,' Jude, her eyes filled with tears, said softly.

To lose a child had to be the ultimate tragedy—no wonder the poor woman had been driven to making crude and wild accusations.

'Tragic was being seduced and left pregnant when she was seventeen.'

'Seventeen—but that can't be right?' Jude turned to Luca confidently expecting to hear his denial; his silence sent an icy chill through her body. *'Seventeen?'* she whispered hoarsely. 'And you were…?'

'He was eight years older! Not that we even knew who the father was until after she'd died and we read her diary. It told it all—how he'd seduced her and deserted her when she told him she was pregnant.'

Jude felt as if her world was falling apart around her ears.

'And now,' continued the relentless voice of retribution, 'he is taking away from me the child he never wanted anyway.'

'Luca, tell her…' Jude caught his arm, her beseeching eyes fixed on his stony face. 'Tell her it's not true.'

'Go and get Laurent, Jude. Tell him his mother is drunk.'

'Tell her, Luca!' Jude's voice rose to a shriek.

'He can't tell you because it's true.' And leaving Jude momentarily speechless, Natalia Corradi stormed away in bitter triumph.

Jude turned her back and tried to tune out the spiteful comments. She focused all her attention on Luca. 'Say something, Luca?' she begged, frustrated by his lack of response.

'Valentina is not an unwanted child and never has been. As for the rest you will have to trust me.'

'Trust you?' she echoed as though he were speaking a foreign language. 'That's a big trust, Luca.'

'Marriage is based on trust.'

'Meaning I should just accept your word that you did nothing wrong? That would be convenient,' she agreed. Only Luca could take the moral high ground at a time like this. 'Whilst we're on the subject of marriage, maybe it's the time to remind you that ours—' she choked '—is based on lies.'

His jaw tightened another notch. 'Originally maybe,' he conceded stiffly.

She shook her head; he was saying what she wanted to hear, but too late. 'You're not denying that Maria was seventeen?'

'How can I?'

She scanned his face and saw no remorse, no humility. There was not going to be any coming clean, admitting he'd done wrong but had been trying to make amends since. *No, I will live with this thing on my conscience for the rest of my life. Just a take-it-or-leave-it trust me!* Did he even accept there was anything to forgive? Maybe he thought he was above the rules that applied to lesser mortals.

'Strength is about admitting when you've made a mistake. I want to hear your side, Luca.'

His lip curled. 'That's incredibly decent of you.'

His attitude was the final straw. 'How dare you sneer at me? You're not the slightest bit sorry, are you?'

Disgust curdling in her belly, disgust with him for what he'd done and disgust with herself for still loving him.

She turned and began to walk away. She heard him call after her, but carried on walking.

She managed to make it to the tower room where her belongings had been moved without actually seeing anyone else. Someone had already been in to switch on the lamps and turn back the bed.

It was the rose petals romantically scattered over the bed that released the tears. She sank onto the floor, a puddle of cream silk and antique lace, and sobbed her heart out. When she was eventually cried out she unzipped the dress and let it fall to the floor; her silky undies followed it.

Naked, she walked through to the *en suite* bathroom and stepped into the shower. The initial blast of cold water took her breath away. By the time she reached for the temperature control she had almost got used to the icy needles stabbing at her flesh.

'You feel the need of a cold shower too?' Well, if he hadn't before he did now, Luca thought as his own body reacted lustfully to the sight of her naked body.

She stood there like a figure carved from marble. Though Luca doubted any sculptor, no matter how talented, could convey in inanimate stone the beauty of the living flesh. He might capture the form but not the spirit behind it. The cold water had given her creamy skin a delicious pinky glow, but through it the blue tracery of fine veins under the skin on her breasts, with their tight, erect pink buds, was clearly visible.

'Or is this part of a Spartan lifestyle you haven't told me about? Should I expect hair shirts next?'

She raised a hand to the leaping pulse at the base of her neck and cleared her throat.

'No.' She relaxed slightly at hearing her own voice, though relaxed was perhaps too generous a term. Being relaxed in the true sense was a non-starter when you were standing stark naked with Luca Di Rossi's eyes all over you.

'No,' she repeated with slightly more force. 'Compared with you my life is an open book.' Her teeth were chattering partly from cold, but mostly, she suspected, from the shock of seeing him. 'What are you doing here?'

'Where else would a groom be on his wedding night but by his bride's side?' He picked up a bath sheet and held it open between his hands.

'I can see it might excite comment if you weren't and someone might even get the idea—God forbid—that this marriage is a joke.'

'Heaven knows, I'm the very last person who would ask you to cover up but if you don't get dry soon you're going to freeze. But as I can see my presence offends you I will take the couch in the other room.' Laying the towel on the bed, he walked out.

By the time Jude picked up the towel the moisture had evaporated from her skin. There was an expression of resolution on her face as she wrapped it sarong-wise around her body.

The adjoining sitting room was in darkness. When her eyes adjusted she saw a figure sitting on a chair beside the window. *'Luca?'* she called out, moving towards him. 'Ouch!' she cried as her knee glanced against the corner of a piece of furniture.

A lamp was flicked on. 'What are you trying to do?' an irritable voice demanded harshly.

'I'm trying,' Jude declared, rubbing her bruised thigh, 'to talk to my husband.'

'I've said all I'm going to, and I've heard quite enough of what you have to say.'

'Oh, for heaven's sake, don't be a stubborn prat!' The tall figure snapped to rigid attention. Well, if nothing else her outburst had got his attention. 'Everyone says stuff they don't mean—even you! And you might as well listen because I'm going to say it anyway. What that woman said shocked me,' she admitted. 'But I've been thinking about it.'

'And you think flogging is too good for me?'

'I know it can't be right. I know there has to be an explanation.'

'And what explanation did you have in mind, Jude?'

'I didn't have anything in mind.' The questioning note in her voice crystallised into conviction as she stated positively, 'I just know you wouldn't do that.'

Silence greeted her words and frustratingly the shadow

from the lamp fell directly across his face so she didn't have a clue how he was taking her declaration. She took a deep breath.

'I know you're not going to tell me what really happened, because,' she added, a note of exasperation entering her voice, '*you* don't explain yourself. Anyone who *dares* to question your precious integrity is instantly shunned. Well, let me tell you, Luca Di perfect Rossi, it's all very well to be proud but I'm only human and I…I thought I could take loving you and not being loved back even though it just about killed me.' His audible gasp momentarily made her lose her tenuous thread, but, determined to talk for as long as it took to make him start listening, she gave a loud sniff and gulped before doggedly picking up where she'd left off.

'And then tonight, just when I thought you m…might actually feel something for me and everything was perfect, that woman said those vile things. I just wanted you to tell me it wasn't true…but you just stood there looking all noble and remote…' She exhaled and gently slapped both her cheeks to focus as her feelings threatened to overwhelm her. 'You want trust? Well, it may be a bit late, but you've got mine. And if you don't forgive me for being credulous enough to listen to that woman you're the biggest fool ever born! Because you need me, Luca Di Rossi!' she ended, finally running out of steam.

'Have you finished?'

She looked at the tall, shadowed figure and nodded. Well, I suppose it would be fair to say I've laid my cards on the table, she thought, unable to quite believe she had just said what she had just said, but not sorry.

What the result of such reckless honesty would be remained to be seen, but, she realised, holding her breath as Luca moved out of the shadow towards her, I'm about to find out. He stopped about a foot away from her and took her tear-stained face between his hands. He looked down at her, an expression of adoration that took her breath away stamped on his hard features.

Jude, propelled into instant bliss, felt a smile of relief spread across her tear-stained face.

'Of course I need you, *cara mia*, I've known that for some time. I was just waiting for you to realise it, and if I let you go I would indeed be the…*prat*?' Jude laughed and nodded. '*Sì*, the *prat* you accuse me of being. The fact is you have crept into my heart and if you left I think it would break.'

'I've no intention of leaving, Luca, unless you boot me out.'

'I couldn't afford to—you'd take me for all I'm worth, or at least half of it.'

'So this is a purely financial arrangement.' She laughed.

'This is a purely loving arrangement,' he corrected huskily.

'Why didn't you say something?' she cried, thinking of all the misery she might have been saved.

'Like you did?' he suggested drily. 'Not once did you say you loved me; you acted like I was a sex object.'

Jude giggled at his indignant expression. 'Well, you are, but I love you for your beautiful mind too.'

With a growl he drew her to him and kissed her hair, the curve of her neck, the tip of her nose, before finding her mouth. With a sigh of pleasure Jude wound her arms around his neck and gave herself up to the kiss.

'This is our wedding night…?' she murmured in shocked discovery when they drew apart. 'Gosh, this morning seems a lifetime ago,' she mused.

Luca nodded as his hands continued to move constantly over her, as though he couldn't bear not to be touching her. 'This is our wedding night—I think it is almost obligatory to make love.'

'Well, if it's obligatory…' Her laughing shriek as he swept her off her feet was smothered by his lips.

'You're awake?' Luca asked, picking a rose petal from her hair.

Jude opened her eyes and stretched lazily. 'Have you been asleep at all?'

'I prefer watching you.'

The unqualified love shining in his incredible eyes made her sigh with amazed contentment. How did I get this lucky?

'About Valentina.'

A shadow appeared in her eyes as she raised a finger to his lips. 'You don't have to tell me, Luca.'

'I want to,' he said, taking her hand and kissing the palm. 'What I am telling you is known by only one other person and it must never leave this room,' he told her solemnly. 'The fact is Valentina is not my daughter; I never even met her mother.'

Jude gasped. 'She isn't your daughter—then who…?'

'I am not trying to excuse what he did, but Marco was very young.'

'Marco! Marco is Valentina's father.' Jude was stunned by this revelation.

Luca nodded. 'When the Corradis approached me I realised immediately what must have happened. It wasn't the first time that Marco had used my name, though parking tickets and speeding fines were not quite in this league.'

'But why didn't he own up? Why let you bring up his child?'

'When I confronted him he admitted everything. As far as he was concerned he'd had a one-night stand. When the girl told him she was pregnant he'd panicked. His mother has always idolised him and he was terrified of her finding out.'

'So you took responsibility for his mistake.'

'It wasn't a mistake, *cara*, it was a baby,' he corrected in a gentle voice that made her eyes fill. 'Marco was not in a position to bring up a child either emotionally or financially. If I had told the truth what would have happened to Valentina? She is a Di Rossi.'

'So you kept quiet.'

'The Corradis didn't make waves then as they will now, because they didn't want the precious *family name* dragged through the mud. They hushed up the suicide for the same reason, and were only too glad to hand over the baby to me. I may be on shaky moral ground…lies are wrong, but the truth can be cruel, Jude,' he reflected grimly. 'And no child should have to live with a father's rejection.'

Like you did, my darling, she thought, smoothing the hair from his forehead with a loving hand. 'Anyone who questions your integrity will have me to answer to,' she announced fiercely as she caught hold of his dark head and pressed her lips to his.

'As far as everyone is concerned she is my daughter.'

'*Our* daughter,' Jude corrected huskily. She shot him a questioning look from under her lashes. '*Our* family. Some people might think that four children is enough to be going on with…'

'And do you care what people think?' he asked, drawing her soft, pliant body on top of him.

'Not any more!' she discovered happily. 'I would like to have your baby, Luca.'

She was crestfallen to see that Luca did not look particularly gladdened by her shy disclosure. 'I want a child, Jude, you know that, but this is not something you should be doing for me. If it is too soon for you…I am prepared to wait.'

The cloud vanished from her face. 'I'm not,' she told him simply.

With a groan he drew her to him. 'It might not happen straight away,' he warned her as his breath fanned across her lips.

'Think of all the fun we'll have trying.'

'Later I'll think, now I need you.'

Jude, who could find no fault with this plan, gave herself up to the wonder she had discovered in his arms.

UNEXPECTED BABIES
One night, one pregnancy!

These four men may be from all over the world–
Italy, a Desert Kingdom, Britain and Argentina–
but there's one thing they all have in common....

When their mistresses fall pregnant after
one passionate night, an illegitimate heir is
unthinkable. The mothers-to-be will become
convenient wives!

**Look for all of the fabulous stories
available in April:**

Androletti's Mistress #49
by MELANIE MILBURNE

**The Desert King's
Pregnant Bride** #50
by ANNIE WEST

The Pregnancy Secret #51
by MAGGIE COX

The Vásquez Mistress #52
by SARAH MORGAN

HARLEQUIN *Presents*

International Billionaires

*Life is a game of power and pleasure.
And these men play to win!*

THE FRENCH TYCOON'S PREGNANT MISTRESS
by **Abby Green**

As mistress to French tycoon Pascal Lévêque,
innocent Alana learns just how much pleasure can
be had in the bedroom. But now she's pregnant,
and Pascal vows he'll take her up the aisle!

Book #2814

Available April 2009

Eight volumes in all to collect!

REQUEST YOUR FREE BOOKS!

2 FREE NOVELS
PLUS 2
FREE GIFTS!

YES! Please send me 2 FREE Harlequin Presents® novels and my 2 FREE gifts (gifts are worth about $10). After receiving them, if I don't wish to receive any more books, I can return the shipping statement marked "cancel". If I don't cancel, I will receive 6 brand-new novels every month and be billed just $4.05 per book in the U.S. or $4.74 per book in Canada, plus 25¢ shipping and handling per book and applicable taxes, if any*. That's a savings of close to 15% off the cover price! I understand that accepting the 2 free books and gifts places me under no obligation to buy anything. I can always return a shipment and cancel at any time. Even if I never buy another book, the two free books and gifts are mine to keep forever.

106 HDN ERRW   306 HDN ERRL

Name	(PLEASE PRINT)	
Address		Apt. #
City	State/Prov.	Zip/Postal Code

Signature (if under 18, a parent or guardian must sign)

Mail to the Harlequin Reader Service:
IN U.S.A.: P.O. Box 1867, Buffalo, NY 14240-1867
IN CANADA: P.O. Box 609, Fort Erie, Ontario L2A 5X3

Not valid to current subscribers of Harlequin Presents books.

Want to try two free books from another line?
Call 1-800-873-8635 or visit www.morefreebooks.com.

* Terms and prices subject to change without notice. N.Y. residents add applicable sales tax. Canadian residents will be charged applicable provincial taxes and GST. Offer not valid in Quebec. This offer is limited to one order per household. All orders subject to approval. Credit or debit balances in a customer's account(s) may be offset by any other outstanding balance owed by or to the customer. Please allow 4 to 6 weeks for delivery. Offer available while quantities last.

Your Privacy: Harlequin Books is committed to protecting your privacy. Our Privacy Policy is available online at www.eHarlequin.com or upon request from the Reader Service. From time to time we make our lists of customers available to reputable third parties who may have a product or service of interest to you. If you would prefer we not share your name and address, please check here.

HP08R

*Sicilian by name…scandalous,
scorching and seductive by nature!*

CAPTIVE AT THE SICILIAN BILLIONAIRE'S COMMAND
by **Penny Jordan**

Three darkly handsome Leopardi men must hunt down
their missing heir. It is their duty–as Sicilians, as sons,
as brothers! The scandal and seduction they will leave in
their wake is just the beginning….

Book #2811

Available April 2009

**Look out for the next two stories in this
fabulous new trilogy from Penny Jordan:**

THE SICILIAN BOSS'S MISTRESS in May
THE SICILIAN'S BABY BARGAIN in August